TEMPTATION

DARK TALES

SADIE KING

TEMPTATION

An explosive instalove retelling of Hansel and Gretel where the witch is a damaged hero and the house of candy is a pleasure den...

She stumbled into my cabin lost and pursued and needing shelter. I took her in, but one look at Greta and I can't let her leave.

She's mine and I'll do whatever it takes to keep her. Even if it means trapping her in my cabin.

Greta seeks safety from those that pursue her, but what I offer is a different kind of dangerous. The kind that will ruin her innocence and bring me to my knees.

As she gives into temptation, my heart gives into her.

But can a curvy woman like Greta ever love a damaged man like me?

Temptation is a steamy age-gap instalove romance

featuring an obsessed OTT hero who will do anything to keep his curvy innocent woman.

A contemporary retelling of the Hansel and Gretel fairy tale.

GRETA

A branch jabs into my back, and my cheek stings from where I scraped it darting into the forest. The thicket I'm half crouched behind reaches with thorny tendrils to catch in my sweater and tangle in my hair.

"Come out, come out…"

There's the dull thwack of a blunt instrument hitting a tree trunk, the baseball bat Chad and his friends were using to hit pinecones into the lake.

The sound makes my pulse skyrocket with fear and my heart beat so loudly I'm sure they'll hear it thumping against my rib cage.

"I just want to talk…"

"Is that what you're calling it?" one of the other men jeers, and there's laughter. Drunken laughter that makes my stomach drop.

Car lights swing around to shine into the forest,

sweeping over the bush I'm hiding behind. I have to move. Now. Before they find me.

The thought of what these drunk men will do to me if they catch me has my legs moving. I dart away from the bush and head in the only direction that feels safe, deeper into the forest.

There's a shout behind me and the sound of branches breaking as Chad pursues me.

The light from the car casts elongated shadows into my path, making the trees rise toward me in sinister figure-like shapes, their spindly arms reaching for me.

My heart's pumping like a scared rabbit, and I cover my mouth to stop from crying out. Fear moves my legs as I run blindly. Branches scrape my skin and catch in my sweater. I keep going, the sweater tugging free as the fabric tears.

It's my favorite red fitted sweater, the last one Mom knitted for me, that I shrugged over my best casual jeans, knowing how well it accentuated my curves in a casual, not trying too hard kind of a way.

Stupid girl.

It seems like a lifetime ago, packing for a camping trip with a man I hoped might be the one I'd finally lose my v-card to. Trying on outfits and discarding them until clothes littered the bed of the cabin I share with my brother.

I was thankful that Hans was out, gone for a drink at the lodge, or he would have tried to stop me from going. My overprotective brother has felt responsible for me since our parents passed. But his protectiveness is suffocating and I leapt at the chance to get away from his watchful gaze, leaving a quick note rather than sending a text so he couldn't forbid me from going.

He would have been right for once.

Chad is one of the tourists staying at the Lodge for a boys weekend, and he seemed friendly when I waited their table the last few nights. We hung out a little yesterday, and when he invited me for a camping trip I ignored the warning in my gut at his smirk and the way his friend chuckled when I accepted.

He's a friendly guy here on a break from college. How harmful could he be?

Which shows how much I know about men. Which is what Hans is always trying to tell me.

Thoughts of my brother have me pulling my phone out of my pocket. The light of the phone gives my location away, and a shout goes up from behind me.

"Shit."

But it's worth the risk. I speed dial Hans, and it takes forever to connect. The ring tone is a relief. If I can tell him where we are, the parking lot by the lake and the path I ran down, he'll find a way to get here. If my pursuers know my six foot five, broad-shouldered Scandinavian brother was on his way, they'd leave me alone, wouldn't they?

I hold the phone to my ear, blocking out some of the light as I dash through the forest. The foliage below meets with a path and I take it, hoping like hell it doesn't loop back around to the front of the lake.

The ringing seems to last forever, and my heart's in my throat as I will Hans to pick up.

He doesn't.

The phone clicks to the familiar pre-recorded message. The sound of Hans's cheerful voice still tinted with his Swedish accent even though we've lived here for fourteen years. I swear he puts it on for effect to impress the girls who flock to him. I was younger when we immigrated to the US, and there's no trace of the homeland in the way I speak.

The message cuts off unexpectedly, and I pull the phone from my ear. The call's been disconnected.

There's no signal.

"Shit." My heart hammers in my chest, and I don't know if I can keep running. But with no way to contact Hans, I have to.

"No one makes a fool out of me," Chad calls from somewhere behind me.

So that's what this is all about. I refused to get physical with Chad because he's had too much to drink, and the charming college student I met at The Lodge turned into a lascivious drunk who was getting too handsy. I told him no, probably not a word he's used to hearing, and now he wants to teach me a lesson.

I've been running along the path so I don't trip over anything, but if I want to get away, my best chance is to lose him in the forest.

I pocket my phone and plunge into the woods. The car lights are faint behind me, which means the lake is to my left. I veer right between two tall pines and zig zag through the forest, darting between thick trees until the sounds of the voices are far behind me and I can't see the car lights.

My heart is beating so hard my chest hurts. But I don't stop running.

Further and further I plunge into the woods and into complete darkness, not knowing where I am going but needing to get as far away from the men as possible.

The undergrowth catches on my jeans and roots trip me up. I stumble more than once, hitting the ground when a large root catches on my foot. But I don't stop. I pick myself up and keep going.

It's only when my chest threatens to explode and I double over panting that I stop.

Breathing hard with my hands on my knees, I listen to the sounds of the forest. It's hard to hear above my ragged breathing, but I make out the call of an owl and the gentle rustle of leaves as the breeze sweeps through the forest.

I've lost them.

Relief floods me, and I lean against the trunk of a study sycamore. A creature scurries in the undergrowth, and a new fear seizes me. There're black bears in the Wild Heart Mountains, as well as bobcats and coyotes.

"Never venture into the forest on your own," Hans always warned me. *"Not without your phone and bear spray."*

At least I have my phone. If I can get to a place with signal, I'll be able to try Hans again or navigate my way home. But when I reach into my back pocket, it's empty.

I search the ground around me, crouching on my knees to pat the undergrowth. But it's no use. My phone must have slipped out of my pocket when I stumbled.

I'm alone and lost in the middle of the woods in the middle of the night with no idea where I am and no way to get home.

2

GRETA

*M*y arms fold over my belly as it rumbles yet again. I haven't eaten since the bag of Doritos that Chad handed around at the lake. He talked about cooking sausages over the campfire, but no food materialized. Only more beer.

The canopy of trees clears briefly, and I look upwards. The moon has moved in the sky, which means I must have been out here for at least a few hours.

I sink to the ground, resting my back against a thick trunk. Wind whips through the trees, and my body shivers. Not a small shiver but one that shakes my bones and rattles my teeth.

I should find shelter, pull some branches together and huddle under them until dawn. But it's too damn cold. Late fall is not a good time to be wandering the woods at night in nothing but a sweater and jeans.

I wish I'd paid more attention to the night sky. Hans

7

is the outdoorsy one. I bet he'd be able to navigate back to the lodge by looking at the position of the constellations. But to me, they're just twinkling lights. There's not many of them out tonight, and as I sigh up at them, hoping for a guiding light, a cloud moves over the sky, covering the few remaining stars and making it almost pitch black.

As if on cue, a large raindrop splashes my cheek.

"Shit."

I dip my head and pull my knees up to my chest. My arms wrap around myself, trying to make as small as possible a target for the rain.

Once it starts, the rain comes hard and fast. I'm drenched within moments, my hair sticking to my cheeks and my sweater soaked right through. I hug myself closer but the rain is cold, and in a few minutes I'm shaking as the cold penetrates my bones.

I have to keep moving, or I'll freeze to death. And I will not die in these woods because some entitled asshole didn't get laid like he thought he was going to.

But it's hard to find the energy to move. My bones are weary, and I want nothing more than to curl up and stay at the base of the tree.

So Hans can find your body in the morning.

The thought of my brother has me moving. We already lost our parents. I have to survive this, or he'll be completely alone.

I use the back of the tree to push myself to my feet. Placing one foot in front of the other, I walk.

More time passes, although I'm not sure how long, before the rain stops. My clothing is soaked through and my teeth knock together with cold, but I keep walking through the forest, not knowing if I'm going in circles or heading for more danger. I don't care. I need to keep moving to keep my blood flowing.

I'm so numb with cold that it takes me a moment to see the red glow up ahead. I squint through the forest until it comes into focus. A red light. My feet move toward it, and I stumble out of the forest and onto a concrete driveway.

Cold and hunger propel me forward, following the wide driveway lit with red lights as relief penetrates my bones and fills me with hope.

The path tuns through the forest, and as I come around the corner, a building comes into view.

It looks out of place in the forest, a modern house made of dark square wood. There are no windows on the ground floor, and an apex on the top level has tinted glass and a wraparound balcony.

It must be one of the lake houses that the rich use as vacation homes. But there's something sinister about it, the lack of windows and the red lights framing the door.

Outside, a number of cars are parked in an area to the left. The lights pick up a shiny Jaguar and a sleek Mercedes. There's money here, and after my encounter with Chad, a pang of warning clenches my stomach.

There's the faint vibration of music coming from

inside. Whoever lives here is up. I stumble towards the cabin. I don't care who lives here. I need shelter.

I lift my hand to knock and pause as the music swells. There's an insistent beat to it, a steady bass that rattles the floor and makes me wonder about who's inside. By the number of cars and the music, they must be having a party.

A gust of wind whips through the trees and crashes my soaking sweater into my back, making me shiver with cold.

I don't bother knocking. I need shelter and I need it now.

Turning the brass handle, I push open the door and step inside.

I'm looking down a long corridor. It's lit only with red lights attached to the walls every few feet. The carpet is deep red and lush, and I drip water all over it. But it's the walls that get my attention.

They're lined in opulent fabric that swirls into spiral patterns. My hand goes to the wall because I can't resist, and my eyes close as I run my fingers along the patterns. The irregular weave of the fabric make my fingertips tingle.

The muffled vibrations of slow and steady bass send vibrations through my body. It's low and sensual, and if I wasn't so damn cold, it might make me shiver.

"Hello," I call.

But there's no answer. Whoever is here is probably in the room at the end of the corridor, behind the closed door where the music is coming from.

I make my way down the corridor, passing several doors. They're all closed, and as I pass the first one, I hear a moan.

I pause, startled, and press my ear to the door.

There it is again, a subtle moaning noise. My breath catches. There's no mistaking what that moan means. Someone's enjoying themselves behind that door.

The uneasy feeling in my stomach expands. I should go. I should leave, but I'm too hungry, and the thought of going back out into the cold woods has me pushing forward.

Besides, I'm intrigued by what's behind the door at the end of the corridor. The one where the red light shines the brightest and the music is coming from. Unlike the other doors, this one has a sign hanging from a golden hook. In cursive script, the words "Come in…" are written.

A woman cries out, a high pitched sound of pleasure.

For the first time in hours, my shivering stops. What-ever is behind that door is something dark and forbid-den, people being intimate in a way that I never have. A blush spreads up my cold skin, sending welcome heat to my cheeks.

I glance behind me to the front door. The door that leads back to the forest, back to the rain and the bears and the hunger.

Maybe I could find a building around behind the house to shelter in or a shed. Or there must be a road into this place which can get me back to The Lodge.

My stomach growls, and my legs buckle with exhaustion. I lean against the door, considering my choices. I can go out and face the cold and the hunger, or I can open the door and seek shelter.

A loud moan comes from behind the door and I feel a tug in my core, a longing that I've had for the last few years.

I yearn to be touched, but as soon as any man gets close, they get scared away by my overprotective big brother. Hans frightens off any potential boyfriends, so at twenty-one I'm still a virgin. Not that I've ever met someone I wanted to give myself to. I thought Chad might have been that person, a brief fling to get rid of my v-card, but I was so wrong on that front.

Maybe I'm destined to remain innocent and unloved, kept in a virtual cage by my own brother. I should turn around, go out that door, and follow the road home to my brother and the safety of his protection.

Yet...I hesitate with my ear pressed to the door, staring at the invitation written there.

"Come in..."

There's a need inside me, a longing that's drawn to whatever is happening behind the door. I'm curious and tempted and too damn tired to do anything else.

I take a deep breath and push the door open.

3

LORENZO

Flesh moves against flesh, and the woman moans. One of the men slides into her and she jerks backward, her head crashing into the man behind. He leans forward and caresses her breasts, and she tilts her head back to kiss him. One of her hands reaches out and clasps the metal bars that surround the bed. Her knuckles go white as her body jerks to the man's thrusting, her moans getting louder.

She's building to a climax, all three of them are. Even the man doing nothing more than rubbing her chest while his dick rubs against her shoulder blades.

From my seat in the corner, I feel nothing.

Their arousal is curious to me, and I watch as a detached observer watching a nature documentary.

The woman writhes in ecstasy and I put my glass to my lips, taking a sip of chianti and wondering idly if I should tie her to the hook in the ceiling. If they were bound as well as caged, would it ignite my fire?

The woman's face contorts as ecstasy rolls over her.

My finger taps the leather chair, and I flick a speck of lint into the shadows surrounding me. When did I become so bored of all this?

I set up the sex den in the forest to annoy my family. As the middle Berone brother, there were expectations on me that I didn't like. My brother Carlo runs the family in the old style, the way that our father did and his father before him.

But we're not in the old country any longer. We haven't been for generations. Not since our great grandfather was forced out of the peninsula and loaded his family onto a boat in the dead of night. He heard the gunshots rattling through his villa as they paddled into the darkness. Gunshots that were meant for his family.

He came to America because he couldn't go back to Italy. But my great grandmother was upset about leaving the old country, and he loved her so deeply that to make her happy, they came to a place of her choosing. The mountains of North Carolina, to remind her of the hills of Liguria where she grew up.

We must be the only Italian mafia living in the goddamn mountains. It would be a joke if it wasn't so profitable.

My great grandfather got to work. He saw an opportunity where others saw a pretty landscape.

So here we are. We own the mountain passes. The

junction between four states via high altitude mountain passes that the sleepy rangers have no interest in patrolling. They're too busy saving tourists and looking after the bear population to worry about what we send over the borders.

And they have no idea that in the middle of their forest, where tourists flock and bears wander, I opened a sex club.

It's by invitation only, and those that come engage in free love while I watch.

At first it was enough to watch the wealthy couples I recruit from The Lodge coupling together. But after a while, I become unsatisfied. I added multiple partners and then the cage.

Knowing I hold the only key while my willing captives do what they like to each other gives me a heady power rush. But now, as I sit in the shadows and watch the show before me, I feel nothing.

I take another sip of chianti as the trio in front of me writhe together. The woman has been flipped over onto her knees, and now the man behind her has his cock in her mouth while she parts her legs for the other man.

My eyes grow hooded, but not from desire. It's been a long day, and I'm tired. My gaze drifts, and that's when I see the door handle move. It opens a crack, probably one of the other guests looking for a new adventure.

But the blond head that appears in the doorway is not one of my guests. She peers around the door with a cautiousness that reeks of innocence.

Her blonde hair is wet and plastered to her face. Her blue eyes blink, adjusting to the darkness, and then go wide when she sees the trio in the cage.

Her mouth pops open in a perfect plump O.

My loins stir as I observe her. She's frozen to the spot, staring at the action in the cage. Even in the darkness, I notice the pink blush that flames her cheeks.

She's got one hand on the door handle and a leg halfway in the door. Her tight jeans are soaked through and cling to her thick thighs. A red sweater hugs her chest, the wet wool accentuating two perfect mounds.

A pale hand goes to her mouth, shocked at what she's witnessing.

Who is she? This innocent woman who stumbled into my lair.

I've kept this place secret because I don't want the entitled kids who flock to the ski resort to come here. This place isn't for tourists. It's for the needy, the depraved, the wicked. Those who seek solace in the flesh or in watching it, like I do.

It's not for an innocent girl like the one peeping into the room.

The woman on the bed moans and pops the dick out of her mouth. They change positions again, and this time she sits on one of the men's cocks while the other dips his head between her thighs.

The girl gapes at the trio, and she can't look away. She's intrigued. She can't stop watching the show, and I wonder if she's enjoying it. If her nipples are hardening under her clothes, if her pussy is gushing wet. If she'll go home after this and touch herself thinking about what she saw here.

The thought has my dick twitching. It's the first time I've felt aroused in as long as I can remember, and I wonder what it is about the girl that has me hard.

Her eyes move away from the trio in the cage and scan the room. My chair is in the shadows, but I feel the moment her eyes land on me.

She gasps and takes a startled step backward.

Her blazing blue eyes meet mine and we stare at each other, her frightened and me intrigued. She looks like a deer in the woods who's come across the big bad wolf.

My cock hardens at her innocent gaze as I imagine her in the cage, touching herself. The image makes my cock jerk in eagerness.

It's been a long time since I was aroused, but this girl stirs a longing deep inside of me.

Whoever she is, wherever she came from, she's not leaving until she's mine.

4
GRETA

My heart beats so loudly it competes with the music. As if it wasn't strange enough finding three naked people *in a cage*, there's a fully clothed man in the corner staring straight at me.

What was more confusing than the scene in front of me is my body's reaction to it. Watching the woman being pleasured caused a sensation deep within me, a stirring in my core. For the first time since I ran from the lake, I felt heated, too hot, wanting to tug my sweater off and do…what? I don't know.

And now the man's intense gaze is on me, making me squirm.

He's in the shadows, so all I see is a chiseled jaw coated in rough stubble, but I know he's looking at me. His intense gaze cuts like a knife.

I stare at him for several heartbeats, not sure if I should run toward him or away from him.

I don't know what this place is. Does he hold people in a cage and make them perform sex acts for him? And why does that thought make my insides clench in a delicious way?

I shake the thought out of my head. This is some kind of sex den I've stumbled across, and all my instincts are telling me to run. No matter how much I need shelter, I'm better off following the driveway to the road and the road back to the lodge.

Yet…I hesitate.

The sounds from the trio in the cage as they enjoy themselves makes my core ache, and with the feel of the soft walls under my fingertips, my senses are awakened. I don't know what this place is, but there's a part of me that's *curious*.

I've been trying to get out of Hans's overprotective grip for years. Because of him I've never had a man touch me, let alone make me moan the way the woman in the cage is moaning.

What am I thinking? I need to leave.

With my heart hammering in my ears, I dart out the door and back along the corridor I came from.

My shoes squelch on the carpet, and I'm probably ruining it by dripping rainwater everywhere. But I need to get out of here.

It's too tempting. If I stay, there's no knowing what I might do.

But I'm sluggish. Several hours of wandering around in the dark have taken their toll, and I stumble in my haste to get out the door. My legs buckle and I tumble to the ground, my body landing on the carpet. As I stagger to my feet, I hear the door open behind me. The music gets louder and then quiet again as the door shuts.

"Wait."

His voice rumbles through my body, as low as the bass of the music, and rattles my very core. It's commanding, and my body obeys before my mind catches up.

I stop inches from the front door. In a few more steps, I'll be out in the woods. I could follow the driveway to the road and walk to safety. I could forget everything I've seen here tonight and the feelings it's arousing inside of me.

Footsteps scrunch on the carpet behind me, and I don't move.

"Are you lost?"

My breathing is shallow as I turn around to face the stranger. He walks slowly toward me, each step commanding confidence. My head tilts up as he approaches, taking in his tall frame in an expensive suit. He stops a few feet in front of me, his face illuminated by one of the wall lights, and my breath hitches.

He's movie star handsome with a shock of thick black hair. Stubble coats his jawline, and his deep chocolate eyes are trained on mine.

"Are you lost?" he asks again.

This time there's a gentle timbre to his voice and genuine concern in his eyes.

The reality of the last few hours hits me. Being chased through the woods like an animal, stumbling lost and hungry and getting soaked in the rain.

"Yes," I whimper. Tears sting my eyes, and I look away quickly. I don't want to cry in front of this stranger.

"Who are you?" he asks.

"I'm Greta. I live at The Lodge. I..." I snap my mouth shut. I don't want to tell him how stupid I was to trust a man I hardly knew. "I'm lost," I admit.

The tiredness of the last few hours washes over me, and my shoulders sag.

When the man speaks again, it's in a kinder voice.

"Come in and dry off, Greta. You can stay here, and I'll drive you home in the morning."

My eyes lift to his, trying to read sincerity in them. Should I accept help from a strange man? From *this* strange man who has a cage in his room with people having...sex in it? I'm crazy even to consider it.

"What is this place?"

He smiles slightly, and his eyes rack over my body. I shudder under his gaze.

"Why? Do you like it?"

This man can read my thoughts. I look away quickly as a blush creeps up my neck. It would be stupid to stay here. The man's playing with me, and who knows what else he's capable of. He's practically undressing me with his eyes.

"I'll take my chances with the wolves."

I turn to leave, and he stops me with a word.

"Wait."

I turn around and am struck again by his beauty. Damn, are tempting strangers all this beautiful?

"It's a sex club."

My eyes widen in astonishment. I never knew the sleepy Wild Heart Mountain had a sex club.

The man chuckles at my reaction.

"Invite only. I run the place, and I can have it emptied in fifteen minutes."

I can't believe I'm actually considering accepting shelter from a man who runs a sex club. What kind of depraved things does he get up to? A delicious shiver goes through me at the thought, and I shake it away.

"I can get you a meal and a hot bath. You can stay in the spare room upstairs."

My eyebrows shoot up my head thinking about the kind of rooms in this place. The man chuckles at my expression.

"Relax. Upstairs are my living quarters. The fun happens on this level."

He gives me a wicked look that makes my insides coil. I press my thighs together, trying to ease the pressure. But that only makes my soaking jeans stick to me more, pressing cold dampness into my heat. A chill snakes up my body, and suddenly I'm shivering from the cold.

The smirk drops off the man's face, and it's full of concern. He pulls out a phone and speaks into it.

"Clear the club and have the Sycamore suite made up." He slides the phone into his pocket. "Follow me."

He turns and swaggers down the hallway. I glance to the front door and back again to the man disappearing down the corridor.

Every instinct in my body is telling me to get out of here. But I'm cold and I'm hungry and I'm *intrigued*.

I take a deep breath and follow him down the corridor.

5

LORENZO

The screen flickers once as I swivel the camera around, bringing the bathtub into view. Greta lies back in the tub, the bubbles covering her chest and the tips of her long thick legs sticking out. She's tall and voluptuous, a curvy giantess who can't quite fit all her limbs in the tub.

Her head rests on the bath pillow, her full lips slightly parted.

She's so still I wonder if she's gone to sleep. That wouldn't be good after the night she's had. I haven't asked her why she was wandering in the woods, wet and tired and scratched by brambles at three a.m. She can tell me her story in the morning. The poor girl needs food and rest, and that's what I'll give her.

But I'll enjoy her a little first.

Do I feel bad for spying on my most recent house guest? Not a chance.

This beautiful creature wandered out of the forest and straight into my house. That makes her mine.

There's movement under the water, and her eyes flick open. Not asleep yet.

She picks up the soap and runs it up her silky leg. Her hand disappears under the water as she gets past her knee.

My dick twitches and I let out a groan, imagining where that soap is heading. I wonder if she's touching herself under the water. She was definitely intrigued by what she saw tonight, maybe even tempted.

A girl that innocent is probably a virgin. The thought makes my dick turn to steel. How did an innocent girl like this one come to be in my woods? My grandmother would call that fate. She was a big believer in the fates, especially when it came to love.

But it's lust that I feel as Greta leans forward and one of her breasts floats to the surface of the water, the round pink nipple and enticingly hard.

There's a soft knock at my office door, and I flick the screen off. No one sees Greta apart from me. "Come in."

Mattia opens the door and steps into my office. He glances at the blank screens but doesn't say a word.

"The club is empty," he informs me.

"Good."

My fingers drum the top of my work desk. I'm thinking about Greta's silky thighs, her innocence, and what brought her here to me.

"I'm closing the club down."

If Mattia's surprised, he doesn't show it, which is why he's my most senior lieutenant.

"Rescind all invitations. The club is finished."

"Of course, boss."

His hand runs over the stubble on his chin. "This doesn't have anything to do with the girl who wandered in from the woods, does it?"

Only Mattia could get away with asking me about my private life. He's got a grin on his face, and it's the same easy grin he's worn since we were kids.

I don't bother answering him.

"You can go," I snap in Italian.

"Yes, boss." He's the only one of my lieutenants who's not afraid of me. But I don't mind. It's my brother who cultivates cruel loyalty, not me.

Mattia's about to close the door when I call him back.

"Tell Pietro to hurry up with the food. I want you both gone in five minutes."

I don't think Greta will stay in the bath for long, and the last thing I want is one of these cats prowling around when she goes through to the bedroom.

Mattia turns to leave, and I stop him. "I don't want to be disturbed for the rest of the night."

He raises an eyebrow at me, and there's a smirk on his face. I know what he's thinking. But he doesn't dare say it. Instead he pulls the door closed, and I hear his footsteps fade down the hall.

I flick the monitor on and panic when I don't see Greta. The bathroom's empty. I swivel the camera head to look in every corner in both rooms. She's not in the bedroom either.

Then I see ripples in the bath water.

Her head breaks the surface, and she gasps for air. She sits up, and water runs off her shoulders and down her body. She wipes the water off her face and droplets of it shimmer on her fingertips and catch in her hair as she sweeps it off her shoulders, exposing her breasts.

"*Lei é bellissima,*" I whisper.

She's beautiful.

When I first saw Greta, she was like a startled rabbit, ready to dart away into the woods. Now I'm seeing a confident woman.

My hands tug at my leather belt, and I unzip myself and pull out my throbbing cock.

Greta's sitting up in the bath, the water running off her breasts looking like all my fantasies come true. It's been too long since anything I saw made me hard, but this woman's got me *aching*. My balls are pulled up tight as I watch her body glistening with water.

She puts her hand on either side of the tub and lifts out of the water and onto the bathmat.

Blood thunders in my ears as it races down to my cock.

The water runs off her curvy figure, sliding off her breasts, over her tummy and thick legs. Droplets catch on the downy triangle of hair above her sex.

She's a vision, a goddess, and I'm unashamedly watching her.

With my cock in my hand, I tug hard, to the tip and back again.

She reaches for a towel and runs it over her body. Her hand slides over her breasts and she lets it continue down her tummy. A hand goes between her legs, and her eyes close. I imagine the moan coming out of her lips as they part.

I was right. This innocent girl is intrigued by what she saw tonight.

Her fingers slide between her legs, and she cups her sex. One leg turns in as she runs her hand over her mound. Her head tilts back in a silent moan that makes my cock jerk.

Something startles her, and her eyes fly open. The spell broken.

I glance at the screen that shows the adjoining bedroom in time to see Pietro coming through the door, wheeling a silver trolley with a tray of food on top.

"*Merda.*"

That guy's got the worst timing.

Greta's got a towel wrapped around her tightly now. She waits in the bathroom with one hand pressed to the door, the skittish rabbit again ready for flight. I wonder if she thinks it's me on the other side of the door, if she would come out if I went down there now.

But that's not how I like to do things. I'm a man who watches. I've not had a woman touch me for years. Touch is not a sensation that I enjoy. But watching and watching *this* woman . . . I could do that for fucking days.

Pietro leaves the tray on the trolley near the table in the room and leaves.

Greta waits, frozen like a startled deer. Then she pushes open the bathroom door and peers out. She scans the room, all cautious until she's sure that no one's there.

Still wrapped in her towel, she goes straight for the tray of food. Picking up the sandwich, she takes big bites, chewing quickly as though showing me just how hungry she is.

Anger flares in my veins. Who is this woman? And why was she lost in the woods, tired and hungry in the rain? Doesn't she have a man looking after her?

A spike of jealousy pierces my chest at the thought. If she does have a man, then he doesn't deserve her.

She's mine now.

She eats the entire sandwich while standing by the tray and then starts in on the bowl of Galatine's, an Italian candy that I had sent up to her. She pops one in her mouth, and her eyes close as the sweetness hits her tastebuds.

She washes it down with the bottle of San Pellegrino on the tray. I made sure to leave the top on so she knows it hasn't been tampered with. But I could have slipped something in her sandwich. This girl's innocence will get her into trouble one day.

I chuckle to myself. *It already has.*

 Her wet clothes have been discarded in the bathroom, and I'll have them laundered tomorrow. I've left a negligee out for her on the bed.

She crosses the room to the bed, and her fingers run over the plush cover. Her eyes go to the canopy above and the luscious curtains of the four poster bed.

I smile to myself and lean forward, a spider watching its prey.

She turns around to face the bed and finds the negligee I had laid out for her. It's white and lacy, and my mouth goes dry in anticipation of seeing her in it.

Her back's to the camera as she drops the towel. Her perfect round buttocks are like golden globes, and I take my aching dick in my hand as I watch her dress.

I purposely didn't leave her underwear, so she slides the negligee over her body and the delicate silk shimmers as it falls over her skin and clings to her curves. Her hands run over her body, smoothing down the fabric.

Her breasts are perfection framed by the white lace. The negligee bunches under her breasts and falls free over her body, stopping mid-thigh. She bites her lower lip as she looks down at it. The fine Italian lace looks good on her. More than good. She looks like an Italian princess.

Her fingers play with the hem and my pulse skitters, willing her to touch herself, to finish what we started earlier.

Her mouth opens in a silent yawn.

It's been a big day for this one, a big night. Greta crawls onto the bed, and before she can get under the covers, her body collapses. She spreads out on top of the sheets.

I don't know if she meant to get under the covers or not, but as soon as her head touches the pillow, she's asleep.

I'll come down and tuck her in later.

I watch her chest rise and fall, the movement becoming regular as she falls into a deep sleep.

She's spent. She's done. But I'm not.

I switch to the camera directly above the bed and watch her breasts rise and fall.

As she laid down the negligee hem flipped up, revealing the innermost part of her thigh. Her pussy is tantalizingly close but still covered by the thin fabric.

As I focus on that dark place between her legs, I slide my hand over my dick, tugging on my cock while watching this innocent beauty.

She's a gift from the forest. She came here willingly, but she won't leave until I let her. My gaze moves to her face. Her plump lips are parted, and I can imagine the taste of candy on her breath. Her cheeks are unblemished, so innocent it makes me want to weep.

Her eyelids twitch, making me wonder what the innocent dream of. Is she dreaming about me? Of what she saw here tonight? Of me watching her?

My balls pull up tight, and I pump harder and harder and harder. As I watch Greta sleep, one thought pounds in my head.

Mine.

Mine.

Mine.

I say it out loud, screaming it at the screens.

"Mine!"

"Mine!"

"Mine!"

Over and over, my thrusts getting harder and faster until I'm about to explode. I push my chair back and stand up, jerking my dick around as cum sprays over the monitors, landing on Greta's sleeping innocent face and dribbling down the screen.

She wandered out of the forest to get away from whatever demons were chasing her. But she's wandered into something much darker, much more wicked. I'm the monster she should fear.

6

GRETA

Satin sheets swirl around my body, giving me a luxurious tingle that rouses me from sleep. My body molds to the mattress, and my head sinks into the soft pillow so it feels like I'm sleeping in a luxurious cloud. The thought makes me smile, and I keep my eyes closed a little longer, enjoying my half-wakefulness.

Then I remember last night. Chad getting handsy by the lake, running through the woods, and stumbling upon the sex den. Then the mysterious stranger who opened his home to me, with the claw-footed bathtub, the most delicious candy I've ever tasted, and the indecently small night gown that feels like heaven on my skin.

I was worried about the stranger and whether it was wise to stay at his house, but he's given me food and somewhere to sleep. It was right to trust him. One thing's for certain. I'll never tell Hans about last night. He thinks

I'm camping in the woods, and that's all he has to know. If he thought his innocent little sister was crashing at a sex den, he'd hit the roof.

I smile at the thought of my angry brother and open my eyes. I stretch lazily, my head half buried in the stack of pillows. A girl could get used to luxury like this. A four poster bed and everything satin and silk and velvet.

As I turn my head, my eye catches on something metallic and out of place among the plush purples and greys of the room. I frown as my sleepy gaze tries to understand what I'm seeing. There're lines of silver among the purple, sprouting up from the base of the bed to the canopy above.

I sit up with a start.

My hand flies to my chest, and I gasp as I take in my surroundings.

The plush four poster bed I fell asleep in has been transformed overnight.

Metal bars sprout out of the bed frame and run right up to the wooden frame at the top. My head whips around, and there are bars sprouting out of the top of the headboard too.

On all four sides of the bed, bars surround me.

I'm in a cage.

I'm in a fucking cage.

My heart leaps into my throat.

I throw the covers off and lurch forward, grabbing hold of the bars. They're hard steel.

I'm trapped.

At the base of the bed, there's a door to the cage. It's shut, but I crawl toward it and grab the bars, pulling and pushing with all my strength.

But they're as unmoving as the sycamore trees this suite is named after. The door to the cage is locked.

Then I see him.

Sitting in a velvet armchair in the corner of the room, one foot resting on the other knee as he watches me.

"You," I gasp. "You tricked me."

His lips turn up into a smile that makes his face devastatingly handsome. He rises from the chair, slow and confident. My pulse skitters up a notch, and my insides flip as he slowly walks over to the bars until he's standing a few feet away from me.

"Let me out." I rattle the cage, and the stranger shakes his head slowly.

"Not yet."

His gaze flicks down my body. His eyes go hooded, and his tongue darts out to lick his lips. The action makes my body heat. I follow his gaze, and he's looking unashamedly at my breasts.

In the flimsy excuse for a nightgown that he left me last night, my over-sized breasts are pushed tight against the silk. Lacy patterns graze the top of my breasts, and leaning forward like I am, he's getting a good view right down the valley of my cleavage.

My breath hitches. I should pull a blanket over me and cover myself from his scrutiny. But I *like* his gaze on me, his wicked eyes searching my virgin body and the look of hunger in them.

He's my captor. He doesn't deserve an eyeful.

I sit up quickly, and my breasts jiggle as they fall into place. My breathing is labored, and he's making me feel things that I shouldn't feel for someone who's locked me in a cage.

"Let me out." My voice is a whisper.

The man pulls his gaze up to my face, and it lingers on my lips before he meets my eyes. He takes a step closer to me so that our faces are inches apart through the bars. He's breathing just as hard as I am, his nostrils flaring with every breath.

He's turned on.

The thought travels through my body, inflaming my skin and tugging at my core. This beautiful, powerful, dangerous man is turned on by me.

"You seemed intrigued last night; I thought you might like to try it."

His eyes rove over my body and linger on my breasts. Through the thin fabric, there's no hiding the peaks of my nipples. To my horror, they harden under his gaze, forming nubs that I'm aching to touch.

I'm aching for him to touch.

As if reading my thoughts, a low chuckle emanates from his throat.

"I won't touch you, coniglietto. Your virtue is safe. I only watch. But you should touch yourself. I want to watch you run your fingers over your nipples and give yourself pleasure. Slide your hand up your negligee and show me your virgin pussy."

I'm rooted to the spot, his dirty talk causing fireworks to explode in my body and a sinful heat to course through my veins. I'm torn between wanting my freedom and thinking about the trio I saw in the cage last night. The things they were doing to each other as the stranger watched and the way it awakened a longing inside me.

My hand trembles as I place it on my thigh. The place between my legs burns to be touched, and I ache for a release. The stranger's eyes follow my hand as I slide the white silk up my leg.

My breathing is ragged. I don't know what I'm doing, giving into my desires and the desires of a stranger. I only know that I need a release from the throbbing between my legs.

I feel lightheaded with desire, and I reach out a hand and grasp one of the bars to steady myself. The cold metal pulls me back to reality.

I'm in a fucking cage, and I was about to get myself off for the man who put me here. Not happening.

I drop the hem of my negligee and scoot to the back of the bed.

"I don't know who you are, but you'd better let me out of here."

My voice sounds shaky even to my ears.

The man gives me a lazy smile. "My name is Lorenzo," he says, as if knowing his name makes all the difference. "I see you need more time."

"I don't need more time; I need to get the fuck out of here."

He ignores me and walks swiftly to the bedroom door.

"Hey," I call. "You can't just leave." The thought of being locked up here on my own has me panicked.

The man turns at the door and gives me a final smoldering look.

"I'll come back when you're ready, coniglietto."

He closes the door on the way out, leaving me wondering what I'm supposed to be ready for. Ready to give myself to him? Because I almost very nearly did.

I won't touch you, Lorenzo said.

But my heated body craves his touch.

With the man gone, I lie back on the bed. But all I can think of is the way he looked at me, the desire in his eyes and what I nearly did for him.

What would have happened if I'd kept going? If I'd let him watch me the way he watched the trio in the cage last night?

Heat courses through my body, and my nipples are so hard it's painful. My hands slide down my body, and I take one nipple in my fingertips while my other hand slides up my thigh. I'm clearly not thinking straight if I'm considering giving in to this man's requests. My longing is clouding my judgement, and I need to relieve some pressure to clear my head.

But the only thing that's running through my head as I touch myself is the wicked stranger, Lorenzo, and the wicked things I want him to do to me.

7

LORENZO

I run down the hall and throw myself through the door to my office. My heart hammers against my ribcage, and my dick's so hard it's about to burst.

A few moments in the presence of Greta, and I'm about to lose control. My fingers fumble as I undo the zipper of my pants and pull my throbbing cock into my fist.

Her body in the white negligee, so innocent and so ripe for the taking, was almost too much to bear. She's so close to giving me what I want that I almost got a look at that sweet flower she's hiding under the negligee.

With my dick in my hand, I zoom in on the camera on her room. She's lying back on the covers. One hand slides over her nipple, and the other travels down the curves of her body and between her legs. She slips her hand under the negligee.

I grip my dick at the base to stop from losing it. My coniglietto is turned on. That's why she's still here. If I didn't think some part of her was intrigued by the cage, then I'd let her go.

But the way her hands move over her body tell me a different story. She is intrigued. She's turned on. She's giving me a show, and she doesn't even know it.

Her hand disappears under the hem of the negligee, and I watch her face to see the moment when she touches her sensitive core. Her hips buck, and her lips part. Maddeningly, the hem of the negligee stays down, covering her sweet pussy.

"Fuck," I grunt in frustration.

I want to get a peek of her shy pussy; I want to see what shade of pink her lips are and how swollen they become as I watch her.

But I'll have to wait for that particular prize.

She tugs the top of the negligee down, revealing one perfect breast, and her fingers pinch at the nipple until it's pink and swollen. She tugs at it while her hand moves between her legs and her teeth bite her bottom lip.

She's the picture of destroyed innocence. The beauty in the white negligee doing dirty things to herself. She knows she shouldn't be here, but she can't resist. She gave in to temptation, and now she'll pay the price.

The price is her innocence, and I'm ready to take it.

But it's more than her innocence that makes Greta so compelling. I like the fire in her, the curiosity, the strength. I want to know all about her. I want to spend my life watching her come.

But right now, all I focus on is her face as it contorts in ecstasy. She writhes on the bed, and her mouth drops open in a silent moan. My dick lengthens, and when she comes I let myself go, spurting into my palm until it drips through my fingers and onto the plush carpet.

As I wipe myself up, I feel anything but satisfied. I won't be until Greta performs for me willingly, and I'll keep her locked up till then.

8

GRETA

I must have fallen asleep again. What else is there to do when you're locked in a cage? It's the sound of the door opening that wakes me.

Lorenzo comes into the room, and my pussy flutters at the sight of him. With his tailored suit and brooding looks, he's straight out of a fairy tale.

Except he's got you locked in a cage.

There is that.

"Did you have a…" he pauses, "… satisfying sleep?"

My gaze snaps to his, wondering if there's some way for him to know what I got up to as soon as he left the room last time. But his expression is unreadable.

"Yes," I say. "But I need the bathroom, and I'm thirsty."

It's only partly true. I found a bottle of water so thoughtfully left in one of the corners of the bed, but I've been careful not to drink too much because I sure didn't find a chamber pot.

He steps right up to the door of the cage.

"I'm going to let you out, Greta. It's not my intention to hold you against your will."

I raise my eyebrows in disbelief. "Could have fooled me."

He smiles, revealing a dimple in his left cheek. And just like that, he gets even more handsome.

From his pocket, he produces a gold key on a red satin ribbon. He holds it up and inserts it in the lock, but he doesn't turn it. His dark eyes find mine.

"I'm letting you out because we're having dinner together."

I glance to the window outside, and it's already getting dark. I must have slept nearly the entire day, which is not surprising considering how exhausted I was after last night.

"But after dinner, you decide. I drop you off at home, or you get back into the cage."

My mind reels. He'll drop me off at home, and I can go back to my cabin and forget I ever met Lorenzo and forget the things I saw when I came in here. Yet there's a twinge of disappointment.

"If you think I'm getting back into that cage, you're crazy."

Even as I say it, I know Lorenzo will haunt my dreams for a long time to come. He gives me a lazy smile as if he can read my thoughts, and his gaze flicks to my lips.

"We'll see, coniglietto."

I don't know what the pet name he's taken to calling me means, and I'm too scared to ask. It's either something that will make me want to slap him or something that will melt my heart. And the last thing I need is to complicate this anymore with an achy heart.

He turns the key in the lock, and the door to the cage pops open. He holds it wide open, and I scramble through before he can change his mind.

Lorenzo steps back, giving me plenty of space, but his eyes make up for all the ways he isn't touching me. I remember his comment from earlier.

I only watch.

What is it this man is into, and why am I so intrigued to find out?

"Choose your evening wear." He indicates a rack of clothes that he must have wheeled in while I was sleeping.

"Have a bath, get dressed. I will collect you for dinner in one hour."

He leaves the bedroom, locking the door behind him and I'm left standing on my own. My gaze sweeps over the rack of clothes, catching on sparkles and golden fabric.

"If he thinks he can win me over with pretty dresses..." I mutter to myself as I walk over to the rack. It can't hurt to take a peek...

There are about ten dresses on the rack, and each one is a piece of art. I pull out a silver satin floor length number, and my breath hitches at the way the light catches on the fabric and makes it shimmer.

"Oh my god."

The label on the back says Versace. I put it quickly back on the rack and take a step backward. That dress is probably worth more than my month's wages.

Which is why it's so beautiful…

Tentatively, I slide the hangers one by one across the rack, sighing at the sheer beauty of the craftsmanship. I check the labels, and there are six Versace. The rest are Valentino.

My hand falls away from the dresses, worried I might stain them.

I've never even been in the same room as this kind of designer clothing, and now there are ten of them on the rack, all in my size. Where on earth did Lorenzo come up with these in the middle of the mountains?

Maybe he's got a wife somewhere. The thought sends a pang of jealousy into my heart so sharp I clutch my chest.

Perhaps this is her room.

I glance around the room, looking at it in a new light. There's a set of drawers, and I pull them open, but they're empty. There're no toiletries in the bathroom cupboard apart from the spare toothbrush and soap that I've been using.

There's no sign of anyone living here.

My curiosity grows about this place and about the strange man who lives here. Who is Lorenzo, and what does he want from me? I smile to myself. I think it's pretty clear what he wants from me. But am I willing to give it to him?

There's only one way to find out more about my mysterious captor. I head to the bathroom to get ready for dinner.

It's an hour later when I follow Lorenzo out of the bedroom and down the corridor. I chose a gold satin dress that tickles my calves as I walk. The neckline is lower than I like, but it was the simplest dress on the rack. Until I'm sure they don't belong to a Mrs. Lorenzo, I'm uneasy in the finery.

When Lorenzo came to get me, he stopped as soon as he saw me, his gaze sweeping over my body.

"You look beautiful, coniglietto."

My stupid heart fluttered at his compliment, as if this is a real date and not a predator playing with his prey.

The low slingback heels he left with the dresses sink into the carpet as I follow him to the dining room at the front of the house. It's stunning. Wall to ceiling windows look out over the forest. Large trees grow close to the house, their branches reaching out for the windows and making it feel like we're inside the trees.

"It's beautiful," I say before I can stop myself. I don't want to make him think that I'm enjoying it here too much.

He pulls out a chair for me, and I sit at one end of the long table while he takes the other.

A man in a suit offers me a choice of red or white wine. I don't usually drink much, but I choose the red. A little courage might help me get through this date.

I mean dinner. It's not a date, I remind myself.

Lorenzo leans his elbows on the table and crosses his hands, staring at me while he waits for the man to leave. I stare straight back at him. I don't care how fancy his house is. I'm not going to let Lorenzo intimidate me.

"So, coniglietto." The nickname, said with an Italian lilt, sends a flutter of heat through my body, and I take a hasty sip of wine to steady myself. "You must have a lot of questions. What do you want to know?"

He sits back in his chair with his arms open expansively. It's not what I was expecting him to say. My mind whirls with all the questions I have about when I can go home and who he is.

"Do these clothes belong to your wife?"

Damn, of all the questions to lead with. I hope he doesn't hear the jealous tremble in my voice.

Lorenzo smiles slowly. "No, Greta. I don't have a wife or a girlfriend, if that's what you're really asking."

"I'm not." I look away quickly as heat creeps up my neck. Damn him for reading my thoughts, and now I want to wipe that satisfied smirk off his face.

"When can I leave?"

He takes a sip of wine, taking his time answering me.

"You can leave any time you like."

I raise an eyebrow. "Really? I can walk right out the door? Forgive me if I don't believe you, but I've spent most of the day locked in a cage."

He chuckles at my snarky tone.

"Sorry about that, coniglietto. I thought you might enjoy it."

I sip my wine, hoping he doesn't see the truth: that I did enjoy it.

The waiter comes back in and slides a plate in front of me. It smells divine, and my stomach grumbles. I haven't eaten since that chicken sandwich in the small hours of the morning.

"Venison with cranberry sauce," says the waiter.

Lorenzo is silent as the waiter deposits our food and comes back with bread rolls. I keep my eyes on Lorenzo, wondering who the hell he is. I mean, who has a private waiter?

"Thank you, Pietro," Lorenzo says to the man as he leaves.

Once we're on our own again, Lorenzo speaks.

"My assistant dropped the dresses off this morning," he says quietly. "I guessed your size last night and had them flown down from New York."

I stare at him hard, trying to process what he just said.

"You flew dresses here for me?"

Lorenzo opens his hands and shrugs as if it's the most normal thing in the world. "Yes."

My brows knit together, and an uneasy feeling forms

in my belly. What kind of a man has a private waiter and flies dresses in for a house guest?

"Who are you?"

Lorenzo spears a chunk of venison on his fork.

"The man who is going to take care of you, Greta."

The blush blooms on my cheeks. I'm not sure if he means sexually or like, looking after me, but either way, it doesn't sound too bad.

We eat in silence for a few mouthfuls, and when Lorenzo next speaks his tone is lighter, and I can almost feel like we're any normal couple on a date. Almost.

"Tell me about yourself, Greta. Where did you come from?"

He swivels his glass as he speaks, and I hear the unsaid question. He wants to know what the hell I was doing wandering in the woods during a rainstorm in the dead of night. I'm not ready to tell him that yet.

"I work at The Lodge."

He raises an eyebrow. The Lodge is well known in the mountains. It's part of the Emerald Heart Resort, a pleasure playground for the wealthy. The Lodge provides accommodation nestled in the mountains with easy access to the ski fields. There's a restaurant on site where I work, not far from the staff cabins where I share a space with my brother.

"You're a waitress?"

I nod. "How did you know?"

He smiles and this one is genuine, showing the dimple in his left cheek.

"Lucky guess. Do you like working at The Lodge?"

I chew my venison as I think about it. The Emerald Heart Resort is the most upmarket resort on the mountain. There are plenty of boutique hotels and private cabins for the tourists who flock to Wild Heart Mountain, but the resort and especially The Lodge is something different.

It caters to the high end tourists, those who can afford the $1000 a night rooms, right up to the penthouse suits which costs more than I earn in six months. Then there are the private cabins nestled in the woods and dotted up the mountain to be even closer to the ski fields.

"It's... a good job."

The clientele is wealthy. We get some celebrities and sports stars, and most people are friendly and they tip well, but there are also a few entitled assholes. Like Chad.

At the thought of him and his rich Ivy League buddies, I cringe. I was stupid to think that they were doing anything but playing with me. Which is exactly what this man at the opposite end of the table is doing.

Lorenzo notices my change in mood, and he goes still. "What is it, coniglietto? What happened to you?"

I take a sip of the smooth wine, enjoying the warmth it brings.

"Wealthy people come to the lodge," I tell him evenly. "Some of them feel like they're entitled to *play* with the staff."

My chin juts out as I say it, letting him know that I

know exactly what's going on here. I've been the pawn in one man's game, and now I'm the pawn in another. "I guess that's the thing with wealthy people. They like to *play* with us commoners."

Lorenzo pushes his chair back and stands up. The sudden movement surprises me, but I keep my eyes on his.

He strides to my end of the table, coming up close until he's leaning over me.

"I'm not playing, Greta. And you're anything but common."

The scent of wine and leather and a delicious expensive aftershave fills my senses. My breath hitches as I look into his intense eyes.

"This isn't a game."

"Then what is it?" I snap.

His nostrils flare, and he reaches out a hand. My skin pebbles in anticipation of his touch. But he stops his finger centimeters from my cheek.

"I don't know what this is. All I know is I can't stop watching you." His fingers tremble, and I will him to caress my cheek.

"Ever since you turned up at my door like a gift from the fates, you've awoken a longing inside me, Greta, one that I thought was long buried. I watch you sleep, I watch you eat, I watch you make yourself come with that pretty hand of yours. I don't know what this is, Greta, but it's not a game."

His words make me shiver with equal parts indignation and desire. How did he watch me touch myself? My mind reels, but of course he would have cameras in the room. My cheeks heat and so do my insides. I clench my thighs together as my core tightens.

He speaks of longing, and as I breathe him in, his scent, his presence, I long for his touch. My head tilts, leaning into his hand. He pulls it away quickly, but not before I see his trembling fingers.

I won't touch you.

His words echo in my head, and I swallow the lump of disappointment with another sip of wine.

Lorenzo pulls out the chair next to mine.

"So tell me. Who played with you, and what do I need to do to make it better?"

By the time I finish telling Lorenzo about Chad, he's pacing the room with his hands coiled into fists. The waiter brought in dessert a long time ago. A platter of Italian candy sits in the middle of the table, untouched.

Lorenzo stops in front of the window and looks out to the dark forest. From here, you can see the lights of the resort twinkling in the distance. I think about my brother and going back to our cabin and find that I don't want to.

Lorenzo turns around to face me, and his face is in shadow.

"It's late, coniglietto. You need your rest."

His words come out clipped, and it stirs something

inside me at how angry he is about the men who chased me.

I'm not proud of the story. I am the naive girl Hans fears I am, going camping with strangers in the woods. This man is acting as protective of me as Hans would, and I feel a pang of guilt for my big brother. He won't be expecting me home until tomorrow, and I wonder what I'll tell him.

I follow Lorenzo out of the dining room and up the hall to the bedroom. I'm not thinking much about where we're going until I see the bed with the metal bars.

Someone's been in to make the bed and lay out fresh clothes. I wonder again at who Lorenzo is, that he has unseen staff doing his bidding who don't find it strange to make up a bed with a cage around it.

But whenever I ask him about himself, he gets evasive. Over the course of dinner, I learned he has two brothers and he's lived in the mountains most of his life. He's in business with his brothers, but I'm not clear about what that business is. Something to do with importing goods, I think.

My thoughts snap back to reality when I see the bed and the cage. Lorenzo stops in the middle of the room so suddenly that I almost run into him.

He turns to me, and his dark eyes find mine. This close, I notice the lines around the corners of his eyes and the permeant ones that crease his brow. He told me he's thirty-six, which is fifteen years older than me. That thought excites me too. Everything about this man exudes sex, and yet he hasn't laid a finger on me.

My head is hazy with wine, and as I look into his intense eyes, I long for him to kiss me. We stand looking at each other for a long time, but he doesn't make a move. I'm beginning to think I've read the situation wrong when he speaks.

"So, Greta, have you decided?"

I frown at him. "Decided what?"

"Do you want me to drop you at home, or do you want to climb into the cage and explore what might happen?"

His gaze sweeps lazily over my body and lingers on my chest. My breathing becomes labored, and under his look my nipples tighten. A smile spreads over his face, and he watches in fascination as the hard peaks of my nipples press through the flimsy fabric.

All the reasons why I should go back home run through my mind. I can go back to the cabin I share with Hans, pretend the camping went well and none of this ever happened. I'll go back to my waitressing job, serving wealthy clients like Chad meals that cost more than my nightly wage.

I can stay a virgin, making bad decisions when any man gives me attention, and spend my nights dreaming about the mysterious dark man in the woods who likes to watch.

Or I can climb into that cage and see what happens if I give in to my wildest fantasies.

After a long moment, I walk to the bed and slip off my shoes. My heart's hammering in my chest as I grasp the metal bars and pull myself through the door and onto the bed.

The slamming of metal on metal jolts my body and sends a shiver of anticipation through my bones.

When I turn around, Lorenzo is holding the key. "We're going to explore your fantasies, Greta. You're an innocent coniglietto, but I bet there's a wild bobcat inside. Let's see if we can coax her out."

He puts the key in the lock but pauses before he turns it.

"If it gets to be too much, if you want out at any time, you say lollipop."

The fact that I need a safe word brings home the reality of what I'm about to do. Never in my twenty-one years did I think I'd be in a situation where I needed a safe word. I swallow my nervousness and nod.

"I need to hear you say it, Greta."

"Lollipop," I whisper, my throat almost too dry to speak.

Lorenzo smiles. "Good girl. There's an intercom system hidden in the left hand headboard panel. If I'm not in the room, that's how you find me."

My breathing settles knowing there are safeguards in place. This is a safe space, and despite everything, I feel safe around Lorenzo.

I sit up on my knees, and the satin dress pools around me. I clasp the bars with a confidence I don't yet feel.

"What do you want me to do?"

9

LORENZO

Greta's a vision in the figure-hugging dress, half innocent, half temptress. Her expression is a mixture of excitement and fear, like the trapped coniglietto she is.

"What do you want me to do?"

My mind whirls with the possibilities, but I'll start her off easy. She's trusting me with her body and with her safety. I can't break that trust.

"Take off the dress," I instruct.

With trembling fingers, she gathers the fabric pooling around her knees and pulls it up. Her creamy thighs are revealed and then the white underwear I laid out for her with the dresses. The delicate lace woven in patterns barely covers her mound. Pale golden hair curls under the lace, a tantalizing peek of what she's got hidden.

My gaze follows her progress as she pulls the dress over her breasts and over her head. She flings the dress to the side and her arms cross over her body, the bold-ness of the action giving way to shyness. The gesture makes me frown. She shouldn't be shy about her curves. I'll make her appreciate her body as much as I do.

"Hold onto the bars."

She hesitates only a moment before following my instruction.

It gets her hands away from her body and presses her forward so her gorgeous breasts stick out. My breath hitches, and my mouth goes dry. I reach a hand out to her perfect breasts, two pale globes framed by delicate Burano lace.

But I stop myself before my hand goes through the bars. This desire to touch her confuses me. I don't touch. I haven't touched a woman in more than ten years. But when I look at Greta, my fingertips ache to run over her smooth skin, to feel her pressed against me, to taste her, to kiss her innocent mouth.

"Touch your tits."

It comes out harshly, and I turn away before I climb into the cage with her. My place is in the shadows and I retreat there now, to the corner of the room where I sink into my armchair.

I'm here to watch, not join in. And I'll have my damn show.

Greta moves her hand over her bra, swaying her hips gently in a way that makes my dick throb. I've had a semi hard-on ever since I saw her in that gold dress tonight, but now, in the white underwear with one hand grasping the cage, my cock aches for release.

I unzip my pants and grip the base of my cock.

"Give me a show, coniglietto. Make yourself feel good. But go nice and slow. I want to find out what turns you on. What makes your nipples hard. And most of all, I want to see your pretty pussy."

She gasps at my dirty words, and a patch of dampness forms on the gusset of her panties. The scent of her arousal travels across the room, and I groan as my nostrils fill with her. My dick jerks, and pre-cum shoots from the tip.

I grip the base hard until I regain control.

"You make me ache, coniglietto. You make my dick hard as steel thinking about your virgin cunt."

She gasps again, and her hand slides down to her panties. She runs her fingertips over the gusset, and a moan escapes her lips. A startled expression forms on her face, and she bites her lower lip.

"Don't be shy, coniglietto. You're beautiful, and I want to watch you come. Rub that pretty pussy for me. Get her all wet."

Greta slides her hands over her damp panties. Her head tilts back and her eyes close, giving in to the sensation.

I pull long strokes up my shaft as I watch her touch herself.

She's perfect. The way she's letting herself go, trusting me enough to explore with me, touches something deep inside me, a part of my soul that I thought was long dead. That a sweet woman like Greta could trust a withered monster like me, that she could feel safe with me has my chest swelling to an almost painful level. A wave of protectiveness washes over me, and I stand up out of my chair.

The movement makes her open her eyes, and she looks at me with lust in them.

"Why don't you come over and touch me yourself?" she asks shyly.

My heart skips a beat and my yearning stretches across the room. A longing deep inside wills me to go to her. To run my hands over her body and lose myself in her flesh. How coming together might be the only thing that eases this ache I have for her.

Until she sees my scars.

I remember the disgust of the last woman I was with, ten years ago. How desire died in her eyes when she saw what I really was.

No, it's better this way. To satisfy my needs from a distance.

"Take your panties off."

I bark the command and disappointment flickers across her face, but she needs to understand that this is how it is with me. I watch, nothing more.

Her fingertips slide into her panties, and she peels them off. My breath catches at the triangle of pale hair decorating her mound. I wonder what it would feel like on my fingertips.

I push the thought down.

"Spread your legs and show me your pussy."

There's no hesitation this time. My girl is learning fast.

Staying on her knees, Greta spreads her thighs, and with her fingers she edges her folds apart. And there she is, her pretty pink pussy swollen and glistening and aching to be touched.

"Make yourself feel good, coniglietto. Do what you need to do."

She runs a finger through her folds, playing at her entrance. Her palm finds her hard nub of nerves, and she rubs herself as her other hand teases her nipples.

She's so goddamn sexy I can't take it much longer. My cock's jerking in my hand, and I give it controlled tugs as I watch my beautiful woman pleasure herself.

The little moans coming from her lips echo through my empty heart, and as her climax builds, I know there is no way I'm letting her go after this. Greta is mine, and the sooner she accepts that the better.

Her moans turn to cries, and she grips the bars as her orgasm races through her. Her face is tilted back in ecstasy, and it's that look of pure pleasure that's my undoing.

I come with a growl, spraying my seed into my palm in thick hot ropes.

I should have sprayed it into her womb.

The thought comes unbidden into my head, and an image of Greta round bellied with my child springs into my mind. The image, so clear in my mind's eye, brings me up short. Is this the future I want?

"Lorenzo…" Greta pants, and there's need in her voice. She's as unsatisfied as I am, and I need to rectify that.

She's breathing hard, and I can't bear to look at her lusty eyes or I'm going to climb in that cage and take her. And that would break the spell of what we have going on here.

I talk her through another two orgasms until she's spent and exhausted.

Then I bring her a warm flannel, and I leave her to sleep. She's earned it.

As I leave the room, I feel far from satisfied. Greta's woken something in me that makes me restless. She's innocent and curious and good. All the things that I'm not.

Tomorrow, I'll figure out how to make her stay for good, but tonight I have business to attend to.

10

LORENZO

Greta sleeps like a princess with her hair fanned out across the pillow and one arm thrown above her head.

It's only Mattia's knock that makes me turn off the screen.

"You wanted to see me?"

Mattia watches my hand moving away from the monitor, and his eyes crinkle in a smile.

"What?" I bark.

He chuckles. "Never thought I'd see the day a woman penetrated your cold heart."

He's smiling as he says it, and only he could get away with this kind of familiarity with me.

"She's my guest, that's all."

One that I don't want to leave.

"I need you to find someone."

The smile snaps off Mattia's face, and he's all business.

"Who?"

"A boy called Chad. He's staying at the lodge with some Ivy League *figlio di puttanas.*"

My fist clenches as I think about what Greta told me. How he tricked her into going to the lake, and then their entitled asses thought they could have a little fun.

My fist slams into the desk so hard my monitors rattle.

"Bring them in."

"To the vault?" Mattia asks.

"To the vault," I confirm. "But don't rough them up too much. I want that pleasure."

Mattia nods. "It's done."

He turns to go, and I call him back. "Be discreet. I don't want any trouble with Axel."

The owner of The Emerald Heart Resort is an old friend, and I respect him too much to bring trouble to his door.

"Don't worry, boss." Mattia slips into an Italian accent and shrugs his shoulders innocently. "I'm just the Uber driver."

Mattia leaves and my finger twitches, eager to turn the monitors back on. But there's another call I need to make first.

I dial Axel's number, and he picks up on the first ring.

"Lorenzo," he purrs down the line. "I was just about to call your big brother."

My chest tightens, and I sit up. No one calls Carlo Berone without good reason.

"What is it?"

I hear the sound of a tumbler being brought to his lips and the clink of ice cubes. "I've just watched his daughter stroll into my club."

Axel's like me. He sits behind a wall of monitors. Nothing that happens in that place gets past him.

If it's only my wayward niece causing him concern, then it's not my problem. I don't babysit the girl. But Carlo will be furious.

He's as protective a father as I've ever seen, especially since her mother passed. He keeps her in a gilded cage. The girl can't take a shit without a security detail.

The irony isn't lost on me as I think about the sleeping beauty in my cage upstairs.

"Carlo will have your balls if he knows you let her into his club. She's only just turned eighteen."

Axel takes another sip of his drink.

"She showed some pretty convincing ID to the doorman. It's his first shift, so I won't take his job. It's lucky one of my bar staff recognized her."

"She can't be in there, Axel. If Carlo finds out you're serving his little girl, he'll have your balls."

It's not an idle threat. I've seen my brother slash a man's face because he turned to look at his wife.

When she was alive, Eliana was the most beautiful woman in the state. Too bad she was taken tragically early. And too bad her daughter is the spitting image of her mother. Carlo was always a hard man, but the grief made him mean. Too much like our father.

I shudder at the thought. There's a reason I stay hidden in the woods. I hate my father. Carlo may be the head of the family now, with all that entails, but I don't like the way he's turned into him.

I'm a thorn in his side, the black sheep of the family, preferring to hide in the woods with my sex club then embrace family life.

Still, I love my niece, and I can't bear to think of the beating her father will give her.

"Give me some credit, Lorenzo," Axel drawls. "My man's serving her virgin cocktails. She and her friends don't suspect a thing."

"She can't be in your club, Axel," I warn him. "Carlo won't give a shit that she didn't touch a drop of alcohol. He's unrelenting when it comes to his daughter."

Axel takes another slow sip.

"I know. But I didn't think your brother would want a scene. I've put her in the VIP booth and we'll keep her there, plied with no-vodka, vodka cocktails until Daddy can send his men to collect her."

I rub my forehead with my hands, banishing a headache that's threatening to form. Isabella must have evaded her security detail. But I can't blame her. It can't be easy living with my brother.

"Anyone else recognize her?"

"We've got some of the Wild Riders in tonight."

He's referring to a motorcycle club that have their

HQ in the mountains. They're decent men, mostly, ex-veterans who love to ride. But they're still men. My brother will hit the roof if one of them makes a pass at her.

"Any of them try anything?"

"The Prez sure looks like he wants to." Axel chuckles. "Damn fool. She must be half his age."

The president of the Wild Riders MC isn't stupid enough to hit on a mafia princess. He's an honorable man, so honorable that I don't have many dealings with him. They stick to their side of the mountain, and we stick to ours.

Damn fool will probably try to protect her more than hit on her.

"He recognize her?"

"Oh yeah. Can't take his eyes off her. Moved his guys into position around the club. I reckon it's to make sure she comes to no harm. Maybe our friendly MC need a favor from the godfather."

Axel chuckles, but he might be right.

I rub my eyes. This is a distraction that I don't need. My brother can get his own house in order.

"I didn't call to discuss my niece."

"No?" Axel says, suddenly alert. "What's on your mind."

"One of your waitresses, Greta." He doesn't make a joke or say anything which I'm grateful for. "She won't be coming back to work."

"Oh? She's one of my best."

I can believe that. With her sweetness and her figure, I bet she gets a ton of tips. My fists clench at the thought. I don't want her waitressing anymore. Not where men can see her. I'm the only one that lays eyes on Greta from now on.

"You've not got her locked up in your sex den, have you Lorenzo?"

He says it as a joke, and I chuckle along. He has no idea how close to the truth he is.

"She's with me now. I'll have someone stop by and collect her things."

There's silence on the end of the phone. When Axel speaks again, it's slow, and he picks his words carefully.

"I've known you a long time Lorenzo, and I don't get involved with your business…."

"No, you don't."

"But Greta is a sweet girl. She's kind and genuine."

"What are you saying, Axel? That I should stick to the wealthy sex deviants you send my way?"

The Lodge does a good job of quietly advertising my sex club. Wealthy guests who know the right person to ask and the right thing to say find themselves in a room in the hotel where my people vet them. If they're the right kind of people, open and curious and willing to explore with like-minded people, then they get an invitation.

Axel doesn't laugh at my joke. "Yes. Lorenzo, Greta's too sweet for you."

Jealousy spikes. "You got your sights on my girl." My

fist hits the table, and through the phone I hear Axel's low chuckle.

"You really like her."

"Yes," I say simply. But like doesn't come close to describing the feeling that pumps through my veins whenever I'm near her. The yearning to touch her, to have something with her I never thought I'd have, this thing she stirs inside me that makes me want to be a better man.

"Relax. I don't have a thing for Greta. I'm just looking after my staff. She's a good girl. Don't corrupt her for your own amusement."

"There is nothing amusing about my feelings for Greta." How can this kind of pain, this turmoil be amusing?

"You really got it bad," Axel says slowly, and I can imagine the grin on his face. "How you gonna appease the brother?"

Greta mentioned her brother, Hans, the overprotective ski instructor who doesn't want her to grow up. Maybe he needs to be taught a lesson as much as my brother does. If you're going to cage a woman, make it a metal one.

"I'll handle the brother."

"Whoa," Axel says hastily. "He's a good worker too, a good guy."

It's my turn to chuckle. "Why do you assume that when an Italian says he'll handle someone, it means he'll kill him."

"I know your brother."

Fair enough. It's probably what Carlo would do.

"The brother will come around. I have no intention of hurting him."

"Hmm." Axel's not convinced, and I don't blame him. My family doesn't have the best reputation on the mountain.

"Well, if you succeed in wooing someone as smart and sweet as Greta, then good luck to you. You'll have to come up to dinner at The Lodge sometime."

"I will, my friend."

I hang up the phone and sit in silence for a moment.

Greta doesn't have to rush back for work tomorrow. But her brother might be a problem. The more I keep her mind on other things, the better.

I switch the monitor on and lean back in my chair to watch her sleep.

11

GRETA

My eyes flicker open, and the first thing I see is the hard steel of the metal bars glinting in the pale morning light. My thoughts fly to last night and the brazen things I did. How Lorenzo's gaze only made me bolder.

Instead of a blush creeping up my neck, a smile spreads across my face.

I could get used to this.

The thought pops into my head and I examine it, rolling the possibilities around in my mind. I still don't know much about Lorenzo, but I know no man will ever make me feel the way he does. When I'm with Lorenzo, I'm sexy, the most confident version of myself. Yet there's so much darkness in him, so much about him that I don't know.

I sit up in bed and find the door to the cage wide open. How thoughtful of him.

There's a breakfast tray laden with Italian pastries and a bowl of fresh cherries. And always the candy that I can't get enough of.

I choose a buttery pastry stuffed with cooked apple slices that melts on my tongue when I bite into it. My eyes roll back in my head, and I sigh contentedly. The food here is divine. I could definitely get used to this.

After the delicious breakfast, I take a hot shower and pad across to the clothing rail wrapped in my towel, eager to see what clothes have been picked for me today.

I shouldn't love this so much, but the rack of fitted trousers and luxurious sweaters is too tempting to ignore. I trail my fingers along the line of plush sweaters, the fabric so soft it makes my fingertips tingle.

At the end of the rack are the clothes I came in here wearing. They've been washed, and someone's darned the holes in my sweater. My hand runs over the course fabric.

Hans is expecting me home today, and he's going to ask questions if I turn up in designer clothing. The thought of leaving Lorenzo and going back to The Lodge causes a dull ache in my chest.

I don't want to leave him, but how can I stay? I'm Lorenzo's sex toy, nothing more. And once he's finished with me, he'll discard me.

Pain pierces my heart so intense that I clutch my chest. When did he come to mean more to me than a way to explore my dark fantasies? But I can't ignore my feelings for Lorenzo. My naive heart is drawn to the dark stranger. I know I have no business expecting anything more from him, yet sometimes when he looks at me, there's more in his gaze than lust.

My mind wanders to a future where I stay forever in this house in the woods, wearing beautiful clothes, eating fine food, and spending every night with the watchful Lorenzo.

I sigh heavily. It's a naive girl's fantasy. I'm so inexperienced with men that I'm probably reading more into his looks than what there is.

But I don't want to think about that now. I want to enjoy my last day with Lorenzo. If I'm his sex toy, then I'll make the most of it.

Selecting a pale blue sweater that brings out the color of my eyes and tight shiny pants, I dress quickly.

As soon as I'm ready there's a knock at the door, and Lorenzo comes in. His gaze sweeps over me, and he smiles appreciatively.

"You look beautiful, coniglietto."

My breath catches at the way he looks at me and the devastating smile that brings his best features into the light.

He starts forward as if he's going to take me in his arms and then stops. His brow furrows and the smile evaporates, plunging his features into shadow.

Frustration gnaws at my stomach. I long for him to touch me, and his gaze burns my skin like a caress. But he won't break his own rules.

"Come."

He steps back and extends an arm for me to walk in front of him. As usual his suit is immaculate, a well put together look that's out of place in the middle of the mountains. I wonder again who he is and what he's doing here. I'm about to ask when a thought occurs to me.

"Where are we going?" I ask, suddenly anxious he's going to drive me home.

"I've got something to show you."

I follow Lorenzo out the front door and around to the back of the house. There's a path that leads into the woods, and after a few minutes we come to a small building. It's concrete with no windows. A metal door bars the way, and two men I've never seen before stand guarding it.

They nod to Lorenzo and step out of the way. Lorenzo pulls the door, and it opens with the squeak of heavy metal.

It's dark inside and an acrid smell reaches my nostrils, making me wince. I glance at Lorenzo in confusion. Does he keep animals in here?

He gestures for me to enter, but I hesitate. My pulse picks up a notch. After all we've been through, is this another way to keep me locked up? Because it's far from the luxurious cage I've been staying in.

Lorenzo must know what I'm thinking, because he smiles softly at me.

"I'm not going to lock you up, coniglietto. I have something in here to show you."

He goes in first and switches on a light. Brightness floods the room, and I shield my eyes with my arm as I step inside the building.

There are muffled human moans coming from the corner, and I squint in the direction of the sounds as my eyes adjust to the light.

Shapes come into focus. Human shapes.

"Lorenzo…" I gasp as the horror of what I'm seeing hits me.

In a cage in the corner are three men, Chad and his two friends. The ones who chased me at the lake. But I hardly recognize them.

Their once pretty college boy looks are unrecognizable. Dark bruises tinge their skin. Chad has a swollen eye, and there's so much blood on his face that I don't know where it's coming from. His friends look no better. One of them lies on his side clasping his ribs. The other slumps in the corner, unconscious. They're all gagged with dirty cloths, and their hands are tied behind their backs.

I take a step backward, bile rising in my throat. I've never seen so much human blood. It's a wonder they're alive. Unless they aren't.

"Are they dead?"

My gaze snaps to Lorenzo. He's watching me carefully, his expression dark and unreadable.

"Not yet."

Not yet.

"What does that mean?"

"I wanted them to see you first. To know which shitty action from their shitty lives led to their deaths."

Panic makes my stomach churn and the air, thick with human blood and piss, presses in on me. I stumble toward the door and just make it outside before I vomit into the undergrowth, splattering my half-digested breakfast pastry onto my brand new Gucci sneakers, courtesy of Lorenzo.

Lorenzo. The man who can afford to have designer clothes flown into the mountains from New York, the man who has a sex den in the middle of the forest, the man who has three would-be rapists in his shed ready to be put to death.

"Who are you?"

I stand up and wipe my mouth on the cashmere sleeve, not caring if I ruin it. I'm sure he can have another one sent. Bile rises again in my stomach. I've been enjoying the luxury, the good food and Italian candy, without ever questioning where it came from.

I claw at the sweater, trying to rip it off. Whatever this man is into, I want no part of it.

Lorenzo steps toward me and I back away, edging toward the forest. The two guards take a step on either side of me, but Lorenzo says something in Italian and they back off.

My eyes dart to the forest behind me. I ran once. I can run again. But Lorenzo is no college boy looking for a thrill. He has men and probably guns, and there's no way I could outrun him.

My heart thumps so hard it might explode in my chest. Only this morning I was dreaming of a life with this man. Now I'm looking for an escape.

"I'm not going to hurt you, coniglietto."

He puts his hands up placatingly. Those strong hands which last night I imagined touching my most intimate places. How many people have they killed?

"Who are you?" I ask again, taking another step backward into the forest.

"Lorenzo Berone."

He says the name as if it means something. But I've never heard his surname before. I'm just a waitress who works in a lodge. I like hiking in the summer and skiing in the winter. I don't know who anyone on the mountain is aside from the small community at the resort.

"My family has…business dealings on the mountain."

The way he says it gives way too much meaning to the word 'business.'

Suddenly, my brain clicks it all into place. The Italian wine, the Italian clothing, the goddamn Italian sweets…

"Are you…mafia?"

My mind reels. Is there real life mafia on the mountain? On quiet, sleepy Wild Heart Mountain with jovial tourists, cranky mountain men, and wholesome good people? There can't really be mafia here.

But he doesn't deny it.

"Are you?" I press.

"Yes, coniglietto."

My mouth drops open. And I know it's the truth.

"My brother is head of the Berone family. I help out in the family business."

"And what business is that?" I snap.

A slow smile spreads across his face, showing off that one dimple, and damn it, my damn pussy flutters at the smile. He's still the most attractive man I've ever met despite just finding out that his family are criminals.

"It's best you don't ask too many questions, coniglietto. Once we're married, you can learn more."

My jaw hits the floor, and I didn't think I could have any more surprises today.

"Married?" I splutter. "Why would I want to marry into a mafia family?"

But even as I say the words, my heart flutters at the revelation that this is more than a game to Lorenzo.

Lorenzo glances at the men by the door and says something in Italian.

"Come." He indicates that we should take the path back to the house. "Let's discuss this in private."

I can only stare at him. If he thinks I'm going back to that house, then he's crazy. Not to mention the men in the shed whose lives are about to end.

"No."

I stick my chin out defiantly. I'd rather take my chances out in the woods then go back to the house with Lorenzo.

He looks at me for a long time, and under his gaze my resolution wavers. Why does he have to be so damn attractive?

"I will not hurt you, Greta. Let me explain about my family. Let me show you who I am. All of me. Once you know me, you can decide to stay or go."

His look is sincere, and the thought of finding out about this man is too intriguing. I've been curious about the dark stranger in the woods, and he's only shown me a glimpse of himself. This is my chance to know the man who's been awakening things inside me I can't explain. Otherwise, I'll spend my life wondering.

"Then you'll take me home?"

"You have my word."

I'm pretty sure there is some kind of honor code between mafia that means if he makes a promise, he'll keep it. Besides, despite everything I've just seen, I don't believe Lorenzo will hurt me. But there's something else.

"The men in there…" I indicate the shed, and a wave of nausea hits.

"You can't kill them."

Fire flashes in Lorenzo's eyes. "They hurt you, coniglietto. They scared a woman into the woods and left you there for the animals." His hands curl into fists. "They don't deserve to live."

He makes a good point, but I will not be responsible for another human being's death.

"They're shit heads, I agree. But they've learned their lesson. Let them go, Lorenzo."

I stick my hands on my hips, unwavering. If I'm even considering letting this man explain himself, then he needs to know that I'm not going to be a pushover.

We stare each other down, but I don't look away.

Finally, Lorenzo breaks the gaze.

"You have a soft heart, coniglietto," he mutters.

He turns to the men. "Cut them loose." He looks at me pointedly and speaks in English, letting me hear his instructions.

"They are to be released into the forest alive."

The men nod their understanding, and Lorenzo turns to me.

"Anything you ask, Greta, it is yours."

He takes a step closer to me, and his hot breath brushes my cheeks.

"But hear this. If any man hurts you again, whether you decide to stay with me or not, I will hunt them down and I will mete out justice. I'm a bad man, Greta, and I've done bad things. But for you, I'd raise hell."

He turns on his heel and starts down the path, leaving me breathless and hot and so fucking confused.

12

GRETA

Like a fool I follow Lorenzo into the house and straight to the Sycamore suite. Sun streams through the window and glints against the metal of the cage, reminding me of the trick Lorenzo played on me to make me his captive.

But that was only for one night. The rest of the time I've stayed of my own free will.

He shuts the door behind me, and as soon as it's closed, I turn on him.

"Tell me everything."

Lorenzo eyes me warily. "Sit."

He indicates the armchair in the corner of the room from where he likes to watch, and I sink into the plush velvet.

He pulls up one of the wooden chairs from the table and sits in front of me.

"What do you want to know, coniglietto?"

My mind whirls with all the questions.

"What does that mean?"

Coniglietto?" A smile plays at his lips. "Little rabbit. Because when you came to me you were like a lost bunny, innocent and soft, that needed protecting from the wolves."

"You *are* the wolf," I mutter.

Lorenzo cocks his head to one side. "Yes, I am, little coniglietto. I told you to be wary."

He did. He warned me what I was getting into, but my stupid longing to shed my naiveté clouded my judgement. I thought he was a wealthy deviant hiding out in the woods, not mafia.

"Tell me about your family. What does it mean to be in the mafia, and why are you in the mountains?"

He holds his hand up. "One thing at a time, Greta.

"The Berone family came to America three generations ago. My great grandmother was upset to leave the mountains of her homeland, and my great grandfather loved her so much that he came here to North Carolina to keep her happy. But he also saw an opportunity. These mountain passes border four states. They are unguarded routes for goods to travel through."

My mind whirs at the information. It doesn't sound sinister. So far at least.

"What kind of goods?"

Lorenzo chuckles. "I can't tell you all, coniglietto. That our business is in logistics is all you need to know. That's all our women need to know."

He purrs the words, and a thrill tingles all the way up the back of my spine. I like being called his woman.

"Your brothers?" I ask.

"Carlo is the oldest. He's the head of the family." A shadow falls over his expression, and he rubs the stubble on his chin. "Carlo…believes in the old ways."

"Which are?"

The way he says it makes me think 'the old ways' can't be anything good, but I have to know more. I need to know what I'm getting myself into. I can't believe I'm even contemplating this. But my heart aches for Lorenzo, for the troubled man before me.

"Carlo is brutal. Like our father." A hardness comes into his voice. "Carlo's way is to use violence to solve everything. I don't always agree. We don't talk much."

So my dark mafia prince does have a heart.

"But you've done bad things. You had those men beaten. You would have killed them."

"Yes, Greta. I've done bad things." His gaze never wavers from mine.

"Can you stop?" I whisper, because my heart wants a life with Lorenzo. What kind of a man have I fallen for?

"For you, I will try."

It's the best answer I'm going to get, and it settles my conscious a little.

"But I tell you this, Greta. If anyone hurts you, I cannot be held to that promise. You are mine, and no one hurts what's mine."

The words send a shiver through my bones. The intensity, the passion--I want that trained on me, always.

"My younger brother Valentine works closely with Carlo, but even he is not happy with the way my brother runs things."

Lorenzo looks away, lost in thought.

"I'm not walking into some mafia war, am I?"

"No, coniglietto." He shakes his head. "I have some of my own legit business dealings, and I do the minimum for my family. I am the black sheep. I started this place in the woods half to annoy my brother." He chuckles. "It is not wise to make Carlo angry, but it is so easy."

Which brings me to my next question. I take a deep breath.

"And the sex club? Will you still…watch?"

Lorenzo snaps his eyes to mine. "No, coniglietto. The night you walked into my home was the night I shut the doors. The rooms have been dismantled. They are ready to be redecorated whenever you say the word."

That makes me sit up. "You're giving up the club?"

He leans forward, and his gaze is full of heat.

"Greta, you are the only woman I will watch. There is no one else for me."

I sit back on my chair, because there's the rub. My heart longs for Lorenzo, but a life spent without touch is not one I can endure.

"Why won't you touch me?" I say quietly.

He shakes his head slowly. "Coniglietto, don't ask me that."

Damn him. Ever since I set eyes on this dark stranger, my skin's been burning for his touch. I want him to rub his hands over me, I want him to touch my breasts and my throat and my thighs. I want to feel his hands on me and his cock inside me. Am I to be denied all that?

I stand up and peel off the blue sweater, exposing my breasts pushed up against a while lace bra.

I walk slowly until I'm standing in front of Lorenzo. He sits back, breathing hard with his nostrils flaring. I lean toward him until my breath tickles his ear. "I need you to touch me, Lorenzo."

My hair cascades over my shoulder and caresses his thigh.

He jerks back as if stung.

"Greta…" There's a warning tone in his voice. "I can't."

Tears sting my eyes at the rejection. I can't believe I was willing to accept that the man I'm falling for is mafia, accept his violent family and criminal dealings, and he won't even touch me.

I step past him, wiping my eyes, and grab my red sweater off the rack. The fabric feels coarse after the finery I've been wearing. It comes off the hanger with a pang that sets the rack of clothes rattling.

"What are you doing?" Lorenzo asks.

I pull the sweater over my head and look around for my jeans. I don't see them anywhere, and maybe they're too torn to fix. I'll have to keep these expensive looking shiny pants on, so out of place in the mountains but so beautiful.

"I'm going home, Lorenzo. You're holding something back, and if you can't be completely honest with me, then this won't work."

I tug at the sleeve of the sweater. Where it's been darned has pulled it out of shape, and the cuff sits oddly on my wrist. But the movement gives me a distraction from the pain in my heart. I thought I'd found a man. A strange, wicked man, but a man who cared for me. But if he can't trust me with his body, then I have no choice but to walk away.

"Wait."

The pain in his voice makes me pause. Lorenzo stands up, and his face is troubled, his brows knit together in a deep crease.

"I'll show you why I don't like human touch."

He undoes the button of his suit jacket and shrugs it off. It's the first time I've seen him without it, and his white shirt clings to a muscular chest. It would be sexy if he didn't look so damn vulnerable, a look I'm not used to seeing on Lorenzo. It makes me worry for him more than a hundred of his dark looks.

He hangs the jacket over the back of the chair and pulls back the cuff of his shirt. An angry red scar cuts across his skin, the puckered ridges zigzagging up his arm.

"I was eight years old, and I forgot to close the door to the hen house. A fox got in and ate all of the chickens."

I glance at his face, but he won't meet my eye.

"Someone did this to you?"

"My father. The chickens were my mother's. She liked to have them pecking around the yard, and my father didn't like to see her unhappy. Not unless he was the one causing her misery."

Even after almost thirty years, the scar is angry and dark. I can't imagine doing that to an eight-year-old boy.

Lorenzo unbuttons his shirt, and I suck in my breath at the lines on his body. They criss cross his chest, precise thin lines half hidden under curly thick hair.

"I never did well in school. It was too hard for me to concentrate, too much distraction. But every time the school called, my father would get out his blade and cut a new line in my skin."

He says it matter-of-factly as if he's telling me a childhood anecdote. But there's no punchline, no funny story.

"That's child abuse."

Lorenzo chuckles. "No, coniglietto. It is the old ways."

"The old ways are wrong."

My instinct is to reach out, to trace the scars with my fingers, to heal his hurts in any way I can. But I stop my hands, clasping them in front of me to stop me from touching him. This is why he can't bear to be touched. Because his asshole father abused him. Because he learned to associate human touch with pain.

As much as I want to kiss the scars away, I wait, letting Lorenzo talk.

He shrugs the shirt off his body and drops it over the chair. Then he turns around.

My hand goes to my mouth, but I'm too slow to smother the gasp. His back is *lacerated*. Puckered ridges streak across every surface. There's no hair to hide these, and the sheer number of angry welts takes my breath away.

"Lorenzo…" I whisper as tears sting my eyes.

"My father liked the whip. I don't remember what all of these were for."

He keeps his back to me, and I force myself not to look away. I swallow the pity and the fear for his younger self knowing it's not what he wants from me. It takes a few breaths, but when I'm sure my voice will be steady, I speak.

"And your brothers?"

"We were all beaten, but I got it the worst. I was the troublemaker, always the black sheep. I struggled at school, and I hid it by playing up. These days I would be diagnosed and labelled, and no one would bat an eye. But my father believes in the old ways. He had no time for a son he labelled *stupido*."

My heart breaks for this man. The scars he hides under his expensive suit. The trauma he went through which has led him to being all sorts of fucked up. I reach my hand out to his back, wanting to comfort him but knowing my touch will make his skin crawl, that it will make him remember. My hand stops inches from his scarred flesh.

"You can go now, Greta," he says quietly.

The words shake me.

He thinks that this changes how I feel about him. He's shown me his most vulnerable side, and instead of scaring me away, it's made me feel for him even more. I understand him now. I know where the darkness comes from, and I'm not afraid of it.

"I'm not going anywhere."

Lorenzo chuckles softly, but there's no humor in it. "You don't have to pretend to be okay with this. The last woman who saw my scars ran off screaming after seeing me for the monster that I am."

Tears threaten my eyes, and I push them away. I need to show Lorenzo I'm strong, that his darkness won't engulf me.

"I'm not like that."

"I do not want your pity, Greta." His voice is hard, and he half turns to face me.

"You don't have it, Lorenzo. I do not pity you." My fingers hover above the scars and he catches sight of them in her peripheral vision, which makes him frown. "But you have my love."

His breath catches at my words, and he goes still.

Very slowly, I reach my fingertips forward and brush the ridge of one scar.

13

LORENZO

The touch on my back makes me flinch, and I fight the urge to jerk away as I process what Greta just said.

She loves me.

The words swirl around my heart and touch a warm place deep inside that I had long ago closed off. Her fingers slowly trace the skin of my back, and this time I don't flinch.

I breathe hard as her gentle fingers move over the dead flesh. All the years of hurt, the monstrous scars I've kept hidden, and the shame of disappointing my father again and again and again rise to the surface.

Dark thoughts cloud my brain, and I want to push her away. To get lost in the sins of the flesh like I did for so long, watching strangers do depraved acts as a way to bury my pain. To keep the trauma buried while I lost myself.

I fight the urge to run from the room because now there's something light, a spark permeating my dark thoughts.

She loves me.

A beacon of light that tugs at the pain and sets it free. Her fingers trace the lines on my back, and with every scar she touches, my soul feels lighter. Like she's pulling the hurt to the surface and tugging the darkness out of my very soul, purging me of my past.

"Greta…" Her name is a whisper in my throat. The words coming out tangled, caught in the waves of emotion coursing through my body.

Then there's another sensation. Her lips press against my back, and I feel their warmth spread to my chest and through my body. A warm glow like I've never known comes over me, and the heaviness on my chest begins to melt.

"Greta." I turn around, and this woman who wandered in like a lost coniglietto and has come to mean so much to me looks up at me with tears in her eyes.

"I'm not going anywhere, Lorenzo," she says with a steely determination that I've seen in the last few days.

My coniglietto is a strong lioness at heart, and I'm filled with love for her.

The realization is a new wonder.

Greta's hand brushes my face, and this time I don't even flinch as she runs a smooth hand over my cheek. Her touch is like the breeze on a hot day, cool and at the same time heating my blood.

I take her face in my hands, and her skin is warm and achingly soft. My thumbs brush her skin, wanting to feel every detail--the downy hairs on her cheeks, the ridge of her cheekbones, the wet tears that seep from the corners of her eyes.

"You don't think I'm a monster?"

She shakes her head. "No. You're my dark prince, Lorenzo."

My heart opens, and the darkness that I've carried around for years flees like a dark spirit, up into the air and through the open window and into the forest to find a new soul to haunt.

I press my lips to Greta's, and it's heaven. She tastes of candy and cherries, and her lips are so soft it brings tears to my eyes.

How have I been denying myself this for so long? But I also know that it could be no one else. No one but Greta could break the dark spell that held me trapped in my own trauma.

Her body presses gently to mine, and my dick stirs. Tentatively I move my hands down her body, and she moans under my touch, pressing her chest forward and tilting her head.

How have I been denying Greta this pleasure?

My hands circle her buttocks and I squeeze hard, marveling at the soft pliability of her flesh. She writhes against me, and the friction has my cock aching for her.

Watching Greta was the most erotic thing I had ever seen, but having her in my arms, is something else.

Suddenly there's an urgency for what we need to do. I have felt her touch, and now I need to feel her naked against me, to feel all of her.

I tug at her sweater and pull it over her head. We kiss long and deep as our hands rove over each other.

"Come."

I take her hand and it fits into mine perfectly. The simple gesture of holding hands, our palms pressed together, send shocks up my arms. I've denied myself human contact for so long that now every touch is like a mini earthquake, setting my body trembling.

I lead her to the bed, and she climbs through the cage door. This time I follow her.

We kneel together on the bed, and I slowly undress her the rest of the way. When her breasts fall out of her bra, I catch one in the palm of my hand. It's heavy and warm and soft and I caress her breast, finding the hard nipple and taking it in my teeth.

Greta gasps, and her mouth pops open. I thought Greta was sexy to watch, but knowing I'm the one giving her pleasure is a revelation. My dick aches to touch her most intimate places, to thrust inside her and make her mine.

My hand slides between her legs and comes away sticky wet.

"You're already wet?" I stare at my fingers in wonder, rubbing her sticky cream between my fingertips.

She smiles at me. "Do you like the feel of my pussy?"

She's got a naughty gleam to her eye, and she must

know how this feels for me. My senses are about overloaded.

I slide my finger between her folds, and the sticky heat makes me groan. My finger brushes her opening, and I slide a fingertip inside of her.

Greta gasps and she moves her hips forward, sinking herself onto my finger. For a moment, I can't breathe. Her hot pussy is so tight it might squeeze my finger right off. It sucks at my nerve endings, sending shoots of pleasure up my palm. My cock jerks, and I leak pre-cum.

This is going to be embarrassingly fast if I don't get a grip.

"Come for me, coniglietto."

I focus my attention on my woman and rub my palm around her clit the way I've seen her doing to herself. My other hand reaches for my dick. It's instinct to touch myself, but she stops my hand.

"Let me."

Greta pops my cock out of my pants and takes it in her warm hand. I groan at the tender way she touches it, so different from my masculine tugs. Her fingers send bolts of heat jolting through my body until I think I might explode.

"Slow down."

I stop her hand. I don't want to cum until I've felt what it's like to be inside her. "Play with your breasts while I take care of you."

She slides a hand up her stomach and to the curves of her breasts. I kiss her slowly as I rock her onto my palm and she pants into my mouth. The hot feel of her breath makes me about ready to explode. Everything is over-whelming to me, my nerves like live wires.

My mouth searches for her ear, and I whisper into it. *"Vieni da me, sporca principessa."*

The words make her shimmer and her pussy convulses, squirting sweet juices onto my palm. The smell of her orgasm and the feel of everything, her lips on mine, her tight pussy, her nipple grazing against my chest has me so strung up that I need to be inside her right now.

I push Greta back onto the bed and shrug off the rest of my clothes.

Her hair fans out over the pillow, golden hair framing her youthful face, her cheeks tinged pink with desire.

"I love you, coniglietto."

Her hooded eyes meet mine. "I love you too, Lorenzo."

Grabbing my cock by the base, I nudge her thighs apart and run my tip through her glistening folds. My cock glides through her juices, and pre-cum mixes with her cream.

She whimpers and I groan as the sensations course through my body threatening to overwhelm me.

My dick rests at her entrance, and I nudge inside. It's only an inch, but her pussy clings to my cock, enveloping me in sticky heat. Energy shoots through my body and I cry out, almost losing control.

"Fuuck, Greta. You feel too…"

I can't finish the sentence because she lifts her hips, taking me in another inch.

"Fuuuck."

I grab the base of my dick before I explode. My eyes are shut tight so I don't see the woman below me and completely lose it.

I wait like this until my heartbeat gets under control, and when I open my eyes, Greta is grinning at me.

She wiggles her hips, and I grab hold of her flesh to keep them in place. "You make one move, and I'm going to lose it."

That only makes her smile more, and I think she's enjoying seeing me lose control. Defiantly, she puts a finger in her mouth and sucks it between her swollen lips before bringing it down to her nipple. As she runs her wet finger around her nipple, her back arches in pleasure.

"Lose control, Lorenzo." Her voice is breathless. "Enjoy me."

Fuck. This woman is too much. She's torn down every single one of my defenses.

I sink into her another inch, and her breath hitches as I come up against resistance. She stills, and it's enough for me to regain some control.

"This may hurt, coniglietto."

I push into her and feel her tear. Greta winces and bites her lower lip. Seeing her in pain is enough to stop the lust that's consuming me.

I lean forward and press my lips to hers. She stills and kisses me back until I feel her relax.

I pull back, my face only inches from hers. Then, slowly, I sink right into her and we both cry out at the same time. She takes all of me, not just my dick but my darkness.

As we move together, I keep my eyes locked with Greta's. She's the light in the darkness, the guiding beacon for my damaged soul. Inside Greta, I am not a monster. I'm just a man.

Inside her safe warm walls, my spirit lifts, my heart sings, and my very soul cries out in joy.

I thought my soul was lost, but I found it again with this sweet innocent woman.

I look into the face of my future, and all I see is happiness. A family, a home where we love each other exclusively. I'll tell Carlo I want to leave the business for good. I can be a better man. Greta makes me want to be a better man. I want to do it for her and for the children we'll have.

As we move together and her moans turn into cries, my body changes. My balls pull up tight, and when I feel her pussy walls clamp down on me, I let the sensations overwhelm me.

Waves of pleasure wrack my body, and I cum harder than I ever have before. Lightness and love roll over me as I pump my essence into Greta, exorcizing the last of my demons. She takes my darkness and shatters it with light as her legs wrap around me and our bodies tremble together.

We fall exhausted onto the bed, and Greta rolls into my arms. Her silky hair falls over my face, and her warm body snuggles into mine.

I can't believe I denied myself this for so long. But I also know it could only be Greta. Greta found me in the woods that night, and now she's bought me back to life.

I woke this morning a dark monster, but I fall asleep in Greta's arms a happy man.

14

LORENZO

The golden glow of morning sunlight causes my eyes to flicker open. There's a warm feeling in my chest like it's expanded, and I can breathe properly for the first time in years. A smile tugs at my lips as I remember last night. Greta's golden touch that illuminated every dark corner of my heart and set it on fire.

The feelings of release that weren't just physical. It was a purge of my soul. I felt the darkness leave my body to be replaced by Greta's warm light of love.

I see a clear future now with Greta by my side. A way to be a better man.

I roll over in bed and reach my arm out for her. It hits cold sheets and I sit up on my elbows, my eyes snapping open.

The sheets are rumpled where Greta should be.

Strands of her golden hair adorn the pillow, but she's not in the bed.

I sit up fully, letting the sheets fall off my torso. Until last night, no one had seen my body in ten years, and it feels strange to expose my broken flesh. But with Greta, I feel safe. She's seen the worst of me, and she accepts me for who I am.

"Greta," I call. But there's no answer. She's probably in the bathroom.

I rub my hand over my stubble, and my fingertips tingle at the roughness. Since Greta's touch, my senses have been heightened. I long to touch her again, to run my hands over her smooth body and silky hair.

But I should get up and shower. There are arrangements to be made to move Greta here permanently and a conversation I need to have with my brother.

I crawl to the door of the cage and pull. But the metal doesn't budge.

I try again, yanking the bars until they rattle. But the door remains locked.

She tricked me.

Betrayal flares in my heart.

I made myself vulnerable for the first time in my life to the one woman I thought I could trust. I showed her the monster within, thinking she was the salve for my darkness.

But it was too much to hope.

I told her about my criminal family. She saw the men beaten up in the vault, and when she saw the lacerations on my body, it must have confirmed to her that I'm a monster. She must have been terrified. Scared enough to give herself to me to appease me. Give herself to the monster and escape while he sleeps.

Anger courses through my veins. Anger at myself for being so stupid. I'm furious with myself for letting my guard down, for how vulnerable Greta makes me.

My knuckles turn white as I grip the bars.

Every dark thought rages in my head.

I let her in, I let her see all of me, and it was a mistake. I'll always be the monster in the woods. Best kept hidden away out of sight lest he corrupts someone as innocent as Greta.

And yet…what we shared last night felt real.

When we joined together, it was like our souls coupling. She shed tears for me. She used the word love.

Tears of pity…

The darkness whispers.

…shallow words.

I clasp my hands over my ears to block out the foul voices that threaten to pull me under. I focus on the moment I entered Greta with our eyes locked and out bodies meshed together. I think about Greta's light and laughter and curiosity. The goodness she's brought to my home.

Could she really be capable of such duplicity?

My heart's in turmoil. Being vulnerable to somebody is new to me, and my heart finds it hard to accept anything but the worst.

The door handle turns, and Greta appears in the doorway. I forget to breathe, knowing my fate rests on the next moment. If she takes me toward the light with her or leaves me to sink back into darkness.

A single heartbeat seems to last an age as her gaze finds mine. It flickers up my exposed chest with a frown and rests on my eyes.

Then she beams, a radiant smile that banishes the dark thoughts in my head forever.

She's mine.

The smile tells me everything I need to know.

"I didn't want to wake you."

From the corridor, she wheels in a silver trolley with a tray of food.

"I had Pietro make us breakfast."

My gaze follows her across the room. She's wearing one of the casual outfits I sent for, and the jeans hug her curvy figure. When I don't say anything, she turns and frowns at me.

"I'd love to come out and join you for breakfast. But I'm locked in."

Greta bites her lower lip. She walks slowly toward the cage and pulls the key out of her pocket. There's a mischievous glint in her eyes.

"I thought you might like to experience what it's like to be the one in the cage."

The dirty look she gives me has me as hard as the metal that surrounds me, and I wonder how I could have doubted her.

"And if I want to come out?"

She holds the key up just out of my reach. "Then I'll unlock the cage."

But she doesn't make a move to do so. Instead, she runs her other hand down her top and over her breasts.

My gaze follows her fingertips as it slides between the valley of her cleavage. I shuffle forward and grab the bars, a growl emanating from my chest.

"What if I want to touch you, coniglietto?"

She giggles. She's got all the control, and she loves it. It's a new feeling for me not to be in control, and I'm not sure if I like it. Although the way my dick's sticking straight out tells a different story.

"Come a little closer, coniglietto. I want to touch you."

She shakes her head playfully. "We're playing by my rules today, Lorenzo. I'll touch you." She smiles mischievously. "But only with my mouth."

As she says it, her pink tongue darts out to lick her lips. The thought of that mouth wrapped around my cock is too much, and I let out another groan and press myself towards the bars.

The sheet falls from around my waist, revealing my hard cock.

Greta's eyes widen and a flicker of uncertainty flashes across her face.

"I didn't realize how big it was."

The way she flickers between confident seductress and innocent, inexperienced girl has my balls aching.

"Come closer, coniglietto. You can handle it."

She licks her lips nervously, then pulls over a chair from the table. When she sits down, her mouth is at the perfect height to reach my dick as I kneel on the bed.

She reaches her hands out and then pulls them back. "I'm only going to use my mouth, Lorenzo. But you can touch me any way you like."

I press my body to the bars, wanting to be as close to her as I can. Greta leans forward and hot breath caresses my stomach, sending shivers all the way up my spine. Her lips press through the bars to my skin, and her touch makes me suck my breath in.

It's so foreign, so unusual. My senses are heightened and I grip the bars, trying to get some control. She kisses my belly, softly tracing the lines of my scars, getting lower and lower on my torso.

I watch in agony as she pulls back when she reaches my cock.

"Kiss it, coniglietto."

Her gaze meets mine, and again she's the innocent girl.

"I've never done this before," she whispers.

"It's okay, Greta. Whatever you do will feel amazing."

My reassurance makes her bold. My cock is gushing through the bars as her breath trails over it, followed by her moist lips.

She moves her head so she kisses the sensitive part underneath, starting from the shaft and moving to the tip. This girl is so sweet as she covers my cock in innocent kisses from her cherry lips. It's blissful agony. I want her to take me in her mouth, to feel her tongue on me, but I love the way she kisses me like I'm something pure, her favorite candy.

Her hands grip the bars and her tongue, thick and rough, trails a line of wet heat up my cock, causing jolts of heat through my body. She licks me again, tentatively at first, then getting bolder.

My nerve endings stand to attention, and a guttural groan rumbles from my chest.

She licks my cock like a lollipop, sucking the end of it into her mouth and then popping it out into the cool air.

She gives a little giggle, and our eyes meet. "You taste like candy."

Fuck me, I almost lose it at her words. And then those innocent lips slide over my tip, and sticky heat envelopes my cock. My eyes roll back, and I grip the bars hard to stop from losing it right here in her mouth.

That warm, sticky mouth sucks for all she's worth and her tongue moves around the skin, lapping me up.

"Fuck Gretta…"

I have no words to describe the sensations I'm feeling right now. I've watched a lot of dirty acts over the years, but nothing is as erotic as the sight before me. My sweet, innocent princess devouring my cock like it's her favorite candy.

I grip the bars harder until my knuckles turn white. She's not using her hands, and the shaft of my cock won't fit in her mouth.

Golden hair tumbles over her shoulders, and I reach

through the bars to grab the back of her head. She gasps as my hand tangles in her hair.

"Open your throat, Greta."

I pull her head towards me and groan in ecstasy as my cock slides deeper into her mouth. She gags and I slide myself out, but her hungry mouth sucks onto my cock, letting me know she wants more.

She's not using her hands on me, and now one of them slides to her breast and the other travels between her legs. She slides it into the waist of her pants and rubs circles like I've seen her do. She's getting off on this as much as I am.

But I'm not going to last long. The sensations are too new, and I'm too eager.

There will be time in our life together to go gentle, but right now I need this release. I need her to swallow me, to claim her mouth.

I fuck her mouth harder, thrusting my cock into her as her lips slide down my shaft. She moans, and her brow furrows as the hand between her legs works harder.

My balls pull up tight, and the moment her orgasm hits her, I let myself go.

A bellow thunders out of my chest and the cage rattles as I explode into her, giving her everything I am. Cum shoots into the back of her throat, covering her tongue and spilling out of her mouth, giving her all of my sweet candy and banishing any remaining doubt from this morning.

Will it always be like this, I wonder? When the darkness boils inside me, will I need to release into Greta to get back to the light?

I disentangle my fingers from her hair and she sits back, popping my cock out of her mouth. Cum dribbles out of the corner of her mouth and she wipes it up and sucks her fingers, swallowing the last of me down.

Watching her take the last of me makes me hungry for more, and my cock hardens.

"Come into the cage, coniglietto. I want to touch you."

She brings the key out of her pocket and unlocks the door, but just as she's about to climb onto the bed, there's an insistent knocking from somewhere downstairs. A moment later, my phone rings.

"*Merda.*"

Mattia wouldn't disturb me if it wasn't urgent.

I scramble out of the cage and grab my phone from my pants pocket.

"What is it?" I bark into the phone.

"Greta's brother is downstairs, and he's furious."

15
GRETA

*L*orenzo mutters something into his phone, and his tone and the way he glances at me as he says it puts me on edge.

"What is it?"

Lorenzo reaches for his clothes and starts shrugging them on. Any hope of a lazy morning exploring each other's bodies evaporates.

"Your brother is here. He's demanding I give you back."

He says it with a sardonic smile, but the thought of Hans makes me wary. He's the best brother a girl could have, but also the worst. Hans is overprotective to a fault, and I don't know how he's going to react to my new boyfriend.

I do up my jeans and smooth down my hair, then wash my hands, getting rid of any traces of what we've just been up to.

When I come out of the bathroom, Lorenzo is fully dressed, his suit only a little rumpled.

"You stay here, coniglietto. I'll go and speak to your brother," Lorenzo says, in a tone that brokers no argument. But this is my family. I'm going to deal with it.

"No."

Lorenzo looks surprised, and I get the feeling he's not used to being questioned. His brow furrows and I swallow hard, wondering if we're about to have our first argument.

"Hans is here for me, and I want to talk to him. He's not going to hurt me. But he might hurt you."

Lorenzo smirks.

"I'm sure I can handle an angry brother."

I shake my head slowly. "You haven't met Hans."

He's the stereotype of a Scandinavian giant. Six foot five, broad-shouldered with a square jaw. He's got a beard and shaggy hair, a modern day Viking. And he's just as angry as one too.

I know Lorenzo can handle himself, but there's no way I'm sending him down there alone. I don't want this to get out of hand.

"Fine," Lorenzo says. "Because this is your family, coniglietto, I will let you have your way. But when it's my family, we do things my way."

I purse my lips together. It's going to take some getting used to, living in his family.

He cups my cheeks and gives me a quick kiss that makes my heart beat faster.

We walk to the door, and I follow him down the stairs to the front room where two of Lorenzo's men flank the door.

I haven't been in here before, and it's tastefully decorated with plush furnishings and a fireplace. Hans paces the room like a caged polar bear, his fists bunched and a scowl that could freeze fire. I can see why Lorenzo put two men by the door.

When he sees me, his face lights up and he runs to embrace me, pulling me into a tight hug that almost crushes my bones.

"Greta, what happened? I thought you were camping."

He pulls me away from the hug but keeps his hands on my shoulders, looking me up and down for signs of harm.

"When I heard you were here…" His sentence breaks off, and his gaze turns to Lorenzo. Anger flares in his eyes but Lorenzo stays still, observing with quiet calmness.

"I suppose Axel told you Greta was here."

"He was concerned for my sister's virtue," Hans spits out.

Lorenzo raises an eyebrow. "Does everyone at The Lodge think so badly of me?"

Hans drops his arms from mine and strides across the room to Lorenzo.

"The Lodge's best kept secret is that we recruit clients for your sex den." He spits out the word. "I didn't know you were recruiting my sister."

Lorenzo holds up his hands, trying to placate my angry brother. My heart's in my throat as I watch the two men I love most in the world, hoping like hell they don't start throwing punches.

"He didn't recruit me," I say quickly, trying to take the heat off Lorenzo.

Hans turns to face me. "This isn't a place for a girl like you, Greta."

"And what kind of girl am I, Hans?" I can't hide the anger in my words. I've done something this weekend for myself. I found who I truly am. I found myself with Lorenzo, and he awakened the sexuality inside of me that's been longing to come out. But not just that, she's awakened love.

"You're a good girl, Greta. Not the type of girl who goes to sex clubs."

"You don't know anything about me, Hans. You keep me caged in, and I understand why. You've felt the responsibility for me ever since Mamma and Pappa passed. But I'm twenty-one years old. I need to live my own life."

The hurt in Hans's eyes makes my chest hurt, but I have to keep going. I have to make him understand.

"I'm a grown woman, Hans. I can make my own decisions."

"This is your decision? To frequent a place like this?"

"No," I say.

Lorenzo snaps his eyes to me, but I keep my gaze

locked with Hans, needing him to understand. "My decision is to be with Lorenzo, wherever that may be."

Hans turns toward Lorenzo, and the fire is back in his eyes.

"What have you done to my sister?"

"I have given her a choice, that's all. Greta has a choice of how she wants to live, who she wants to be, and who she wants to share her light with. I hope she chooses to do that with me."

Lorenzo has kept looking at me as he says it, and I meet his eyes. Everything that's passed between us over the last few days is communicated in that look.

I cross the room to stand with Lorenzo and take his hand in mine, our gaze never wavering.

"I choose to stay here of my own free will, Hans. The sex club is closed. That's not what this is about. I love Lorenzo."

Hans looks confused, but the anger is draining out of him.

"Greta, do you know who he is? Lorenzo Berone. He's a dangerous man to get involved with."

All my life Hans has tried to protect me, and maybe that's why there's a part of me that seeks out danger.

There's a reason why I went camping with strangers, why I entered the wicked cabin in the woods, why I chose to stay in Lorenzo's cage. I'm attracted to the darkness. I'm curious and tempted by a little bit of what's forbidden.

A slither of Lorenzo's darkness has seeped into me,

and it's opened a crack that feels exciting and makes me whole. Light seeks out the shadows, and Lorenzo is my piece of darkness.

"I understand what I'm getting into, Hans. It's what I want."

Lorenzo squeezes my hand and turns to Hans.

"I might not have been your first choice for your sister, and I respect the protectiveness you have of her. But I vow to you on the grave of my mother that I will love Greta, and I'll dedicate the rest of my days to loving and protecting her."

Another vow from a mafia prince. The weight of the promise isn't lost on my brother.

"You're released from that duty now, Hans."

Hans takes a few long breaths, and his shoulders sag as the responsibility shrugs off him. I've never thought of the burden I've been to him. He'll never stop looking out for me, but I'm not his responsibility anymore.

"There's only one more thing I need from you, Hans."

Hans's head jerks up suspiciously.

"As the head of your family, I need your blessing to marry Greta."

I suck in my breath, surprise making me gasp as Lorenzo drops to his knees.

"Greta, we've only known each other a few days. But my soul is entwined with yours. You've shown me the light when I was lost in the shadows. You've let me see myself in ways I never thought possible. You've chased the darkness out of my soul, and I want you beside me always as my wife."

My eyes fill with tears as I look down at the ring he holds out to me. It's gorgeous, a glittering diamond set on a ring of sapphires.

"Lorenzo, when did you get this?"

"I had it flown from New York with the dresses."

"The first night I was here?"

"Yes, Greta. I knew the moment you stumbled into my house that you would be my wife. At least I dared to hope."

His certainty tugs at my heart and fills me with confidence that what he says is true. Our souls are entwined, and there's no other path for me but to be with him.

"Yes," I say. "Yes, Lorenzo. I'll marry you."

He stands up and pulls me into a hug, lifting my feet off the floor. We kiss, and we're both laughing. I'm so happy I don't notice Hans until we break away from the kiss.

He's sitting on the couch looking bewildered.

"Are you okay, big brother? Do you give us your blessing?"

He turns his gaze to me. "If it's what you want, Greta, you have my blessing." He glances at Lorenzo. "The both of you."

He stands up, unfurling to his full height, and spreads his legs, making his body take up space as he stares Lorenzo down.

"But if you fuck with my sister, if you break her heart,

if you make her cry, I don't give a fuck who your family is. I'm coming for you."

The men stare at each other, and something passes between them.

"Sounds fair." Lorenzo nods. "I understand."

He speaks into the intercom by the door.

"Pietro, bring champagne and breakfast for three. You will stay and eat with us," he says to Hans.

My big brother bristles. He's not used to being told what to do, and I see a future with the two of them butting heads. It makes me smile. I've got two protectors, the two men I love most in the world.

Hans will always be there when I need him, but I choose to stay with my dark prince in the woods.

EPILOGUE

GREATA

Six months later...

Lorenzo rolls out the architecture plans on the table and uses a pewter vase to weigh down one end.

"This is the updated plan, coniglietto. I hope you find it satisfactory."

He gives me a sardonic smile and raises one eyebrow. When Lorenzo said I had free rein to renovate the house, he didn't expect me to throw myself into it quite so enthusiastically. We've been through several stages of plans, and I've driven the architect mad with changing my mind and adding extras.

I've never had a home to renovate before, and I want it to be perfect. There were two goals when I started. To purge the place of the sex den rooms by turning that entire side of the house into a cozy living space, and to make it the forever home for me and Lorenzo and our future family.

I was shy at first about anything too extravagant, but as the extent of Lorenzo's wealth became known to me, he encouraged me to be extravagant, to build the home I want.

So I added a library, a music room, a sunroom, a wine cellar, a playroom for our future kids, and I extended the basement.

We're keeping the shell of the house and most of the upstairs, but gutting the lower level and extending it further so the glass walled library will sit nestled amongst the trees. The perfect spot to get lost in a dark tale.

I study the plans, scrutinizing the updated lines the architect has drawn since the last round of reviews.

Lorenzo watches me patiently. He's said he doesn't care what the house looks like as long as I'm happy. I've thrown myself into the project, and I've learned a lot in the last few months about structural integrity, building materials, and soundproofing.

Along with the shotgun wedding and honeymooning in Europe, the last few months have been a blur.

True to his word, Lorenzo got out of the family business. Everything he does is legit now. At least that's what he tells me, and I choose to believe him. If he disappears some nights after a call from his brothers, then I don't ask any questions.

"What do you think, coniglietto?"

I nod my head slowly and trace my finger down the lines on the plans.

"Good."

"Just good? Then we'll send it back. I want nothing but extraordinary for my coniglietto."

I smile at my husband as a wave of warmth washes over my chest. I lean against him, and his arm goes around my waist.

My hand caresses his arm, and heat flares inside me at the touch.

"It's perfect," I say. "I'm ready to proceed to the next stage."

The next stage is the build. We'll move into The Lodge while it's happening.

"How long until it's ready?"

Lorenzo's lips brush my hair and creep down to my ear, the heat tickling my skin.

"It will take about seven months to complete."

"Seven months." I do the calculations in my head. "They've got one month of contingency."

His kisses stop by my ear. "One month. What do you mean?"

I turn in his arms, not able to hide the smile or my news any longer.

"I want it finished and us moved in before the baby arrives."

He stares at me in shock.

"Greta, are you sure?"

I suspected, and the three tests this morning confirmed it. "Yes, Lorenzo. I'm pregnant."

I hold my breath, waiting for his reaction.

We've talked of children ever since we first got together, but Lorenzo is still working through his trauma, and I wasn't sure how he'd take the news.

He holds my gaze for so long that a sinking feeling grows in my gut.

"Is it still what you want?" I whisper. "Is it too soon?"

"No." He shakes his head slowly, his voice choked with emotion. His eyes shine and a smile spreads across his face, showing off the one dimple.

"It's exactly what I want."

He pulls me into an embrace and kisses the top of my had.

"I never thought I'd have a family, Greta. You've given me so much."

"You deserve so much, Lorenzo. You deserve it all."

We hold each other for a long time until the kisses on my head move down my cheeks to find my lips. Our energy joins, and I'm filled with love for this man. He moves against me, and the kisses of joy turn to something else.

"Come." Lorenzo leads me from the room. "Which room do you want me to fuck you in today, coniglietto?"

I giggle as we walk through the house. We've been exorcising the demons from the sex club by using each room and any residual trappings we find there. There's a hook and a thick rope I found in a cupboard that I'm curious to try.

With Lorenzo I'm safe to explore, to test out my shadows, knowing he owns the darkness and won't let me get lost. We found each other in the woods, and I'm forever his.

HANS GETS HIS STORY...
A RUNAWAY BRIDE FOR CHRISTMAS

A runaway bride and the grumpy mountain man whose cabin she's forced to spend the night in...

Allie

I've spent my life pleasing my parents. But I can't go through with the wedding they've planned for me.

I run into the woods and straight into Hans, the hot ski instructor who's nothing like the corporate prince my parents would have married me off to.

We've met before. Two years ago he kissed me, and my world hasn't been the same since. Too bad he doesn't remember, because I've spent the last two years thinking of nothing else.

Hans

Two years ago I kissed Allie, and my world shifted . . . until her mother forced us apart and made it clear I was no match for her daughter.

When I see her again, she's running through the snow in a flimsy wedding dress and no damn shoes.

I should send her straight back to her family, but there's a storm coming, and it's too tempting to be snowed in with the runaway bride.

But I won't be Allie's rebound. She broke my heart once, and I won't be fooled twice.

A Runaway Bride for Christmas is a forced proximity, wrong side of the tracks, holiday romance featuring a grumpy Swedish ski instructor and the curvy runaway bride he makes his own.

GET YOUR FREE BOOKS

Sign up to the Sadie King mailing list and get access to all the bonus content including bonus scenes and five FREE steamy short romances!

You'll be the first to hear about new releases, exclusive offers, bonus content and all my news. You can even email me back. I love chatting with my readers!

To claim your free books visit:

authorsadieking.com/bonus-scenes

If you're already a subscriber check your last email for the link that will take you straight to the bonus content.

BOOKS AND SERIES BY SADIE KING

Wild Heart Mountain

Military Heroes

Wild Riders MC

Mountain Heroes

Temptation

A Runaway Bride for Christmas

A Secret Baby for Christmas

Knocked Up

Sunset Coast

Underground Crows MC

Sunset Security

Men of the Sea

Love and Obsession (The Cod Cove Trilogy)

Maple Springs

Men of Maple Mountain

All the Single Dads

Candy's Café

For a full list of titles check out the Sadie King website

www.authorsadieking.com

ABOUT THE AUTHOR

Sadie King is a USA Today Best Selling Author of over 120 short and steamy contemporary romances. She loves writing about military heroes and the sassy women who heal their hearts.

Sadie lives in New Zealand with her ex-military husband and raucous young son.

When she's not writing she loves catching waves with her son, running along the beach, and drinking good wine, preferably with a book in hand.

Sign up to her newsletter to receive all the latest news and releases and access to exclusive bonus content.

www.authorsadieking.com